Roman

(Wolves of Winter's Edge, Book 2)

T. S. JOYCE

Roman

ISBN-13: 978-1542553124
ISBN-10: 1542553121
Copyright © 2016, T. S. Joyce
First electronic publication: December 2016

T. S. Joyce
www.tsjoyce.com

All Rights Are Reserved. No part of this book may be used or reproduced in any manner whatsoever without written permission, except in the case of brief quotations embodied in critical articles and reviews. The unauthorized reproduction or distribution of this copyrighted work is illegal. No part of this book may be scanned, uploaded or distributed via the Internet or any other means, electronic or print, without the author's permission.

NOTE FROM THE AUTHOR:

This book is a work of fiction. The names, characters, places, and incidents are products of the writer's imagination or have been used fictitiously and are not to be construed as real. Any resemblance to persons, living or dead, actual events, locale or organizations is entirely coincidental. The author does not have any control over and does not assume any responsibility for third-party websites or their content.

Published in the United States of America

First digital publication: December 2016
First print publication: January 2017

Editing: Corinne DeMaagd
Cover Photography: Furious Fotog
Cover Model: Dylan Horsch

DEDICATION

For the dream-chasers.
Yeah, you, out there doing your thing.
Keep it up.
This one's for you.

ACKNOWLEDGMENTS

I couldn't write these books without some amazing people behind me. A huge thanks to Corinne DeMaagd, for helping me to polish my books, and for being an amazing and supportive friend. Looking back on our journey here, it makes me smile so big. You are an incredible teammate, C! Thanks to Golden Czermak of Furious Fotog for this shot of Dylan for the cover, and for being my hilarious backpack-buddy.

TnT. Y'all probably already know who I'm about to thank just from those three letters, but the other half of my signing team is Tyler Halligan, and whooo we have had some adventures. And more than that, outside of the chaos and fun of the events, he is one hell of an inspiring person.

To my cubs, who put up with so much to share me with these characters, my heart is yours.
You keep thanking me for working so hard for you, but that always blows my mind. You are worth every ounce of effort, no thanks needed.
You are the amazing ones.

And last but never least, thank you, awesome reader. You have done more for me and my stories than I can even explain on this teeny page. You found my books, and ran with them, and every share, review, and comment makes release days so incredibly special to me.

1010 is magic and so are you.

ONE

The flashing red and blue police lights were giving Roman Striker a headache.

He didn't know how the werewolf who was standing right beside the crime scene could stand it. Five minutes parked behind the police tape in the woods right outside of town, and he was ready to pick up the damn police cruiser and chuck it into the trees.

The paramedics loaded a covered body into the back of an ambulance, and Roman narrowed his eyes at the dark-haired giant in the policeman's uniform, watching the body disappear with a dead expression in his icy blue eyes. See, this was the problem with the alpha of the Bone-Ripper Pack. Rhett was unstable at best, a brutal alpha, a dickhead on a good day, and he was also the chief of police in a town that didn't know what kind of monster lived inside him. He was taking notes and statements, as though he wasn't the one who murdered that tourist.

Rhett was a wolf in officer's clothing. Small town law enforcement, so he got away with everything. Rangeley was being run by a monster, and the unsuspecting humans here didn't have any idea how bad this was about to get.

Roman's brother, Gentry, had gone to war with the alpha. Hell, Roman and Asher had joined him. Gentry had nearly ripped Rhett's throat out, and that kind of defeat did bad things to alphas like him. It was a slow, mental poison—the idea that Gentry could come in and take his throne whenever he wanted. That, and Rhett still looked weak as fuck. Hunched and pale, he wasn't healing right. Good. Made it easier for Roman to kill that asshole when his brothers weren't looking. Gentry and Asher didn't even know he was out here tonight, following tips on the police scanner, watching Rhett. He'd been doing this for a few weeks now, observing Rhett's routine, figuring out who he met up with and when. Figuring out his patterns, where he felt comfortable, where he let down his guard.

Maybe his brothers had some bigger plan for this town, but not Roman. He was going to avenge Dad, avenge Blaire, and then turn right back around and leave this hell-hole, just like he had when he was kicked out of the pack all those years ago.

As if his dad could feel his anger, he appeared out of the corner of Roman's eye. He didn't startle at the pale, transparent figure on the edge of the woods who stood staring at him. Dad had been haunting him from the moment Rhett took his life.

That little talent was Odine's fault. She'd done her black magic on him to turn him into a werewolf, and now he was like that little kid in the movie, *The Sixth Sense*, seeing dead people and shit. *Thanks for nothing, witch.*

Dad looked like he had the last time Roman had seen him, down to the same outfit and everything. He stood there, staring, just like the day Roman had driven away from here. He still hated his father.

When the back door to his Jeep Wrangler opened, Roman startled hard. Before he managed to twist around in his seat, the acrid scent of fear mixed with vanilla hit his nose. Mila.

Roman huffed a dark laugh. "Get out."

"You shouldn't be here."

"Well, that makes two of us, Mila."

"No, I mean, you shouldn't be in this town. You don't understand what's happening here. Leave, Roman."

Mila sounded scared, but she was a submissive, at the very bottom of the Bone-Ripper Pack. She was scared of her own shadow.

Roman turned to pop off with a pert, "Fuck off," but he stopped when he saw her.

Mila had changed in the years he'd been away. She wasn't some pin-thin rail of a nerd anymore. She had grown out her dark brunette hair and cut her bangs so they hung heavy over her eyes—probably to hide. Submissives liked being invisible. But she couldn't hide how fucking gorgeous she'd grown up to be. Little nose, rosy cheeks, full lips, fair skin. Her hair hid her big ears. He'd always made fun of them when they were kids. Her eyes looked different, though. In the past, Mila used to have control over her wolf, and her eyes had stayed this soft chocolate brown. But since he'd come back to Rangeley, he'd never seen her eyes any color but the striking champagne tone of her wolf. Something bad had happened to her animal to freeze that color in her face. *Don't pity her. She's one of them.*

Mila was wearing a thick, black jacket with one of those fur-lined hoods, and she was hunched down in the seat, hiding behind him. Hiding from her alpha, who would probably kill her just for talking to Roman.

Roman couldn't figure out if he cared too much about that yet. Mila felt like a traitor.

"You need to stop digging, need to stop stalking. You and your brothers need to go."

"Go where?" he asked innocently. "This is home-sweet-home."

"B-bullcrap. You left on purpose." Whoo, there was deep bitterness in her voice. Roman glared at her suspiciously, tried to figure out what that angry look in her eyes meant. Mila had feelings about him leaving?

"You and your brothers are the reason this is all happening," she said on the quietest breath. "The least you can do is let us try and pick up the pieces."

Roman slammed his open palm on the steering

wheel. "Pick up the pieces by murdering some hunter in the woods? Pick up the pieces by hunting Blaire? By trying to kill her? I fucking saw you there, Mila. Yeah, you hung back, but you were there, herding her, helping Rhett hunt a fucking human woman. Do you know what we had to do—?" Roman cut himself off from the memory of what Odine had done to save Blaire's life. Mila didn't deserve the real stuff. He was a jokester, sure. He liked to play, liked to mask hurt with laughter. But underneath the jokes, he was pissed, and Mila was here practically begging for him to take his anger out on her.

Dad was closer now, twenty yards away from the window, still staring. Always staring. Roman scrubbed his hand down his face. He wanted to hurt her with words because that's what monsters like him did. "When we were kids, I remember you liked Gentry."

"False."

"Don't bullshit me, Mila. You had eyes for Gentry—"

"Because he could've kept me safe! You arrogant asshole, you know nothing about me or my life. He could've kept me safe. Gentry was nice to submissives, just like your dad was. He left me. You left me. Asher left me."

"Why didn't you leave then, Mila? Huh? This isn't on me or my brothers. Why didn't you pack your shit and find a better pack?"

"Because Odine bound me to Rangeley!" Mila dragged in a sound that resembled a muffled sob, and Roman jerked his gaze to the back seat just in time to see her shoving the door open. A tear glistened on her cheek. Before she slid out of his jeep, she whispered raggedly, "You didn't even say goodbye, Roman. You were my friend once, and that's the only reason I'm trying to save you now. Just…stay away from the witch, and leave while you still can. Please."

Mila closed the door behind her quietly and slipped into the woods.

The ghost of his father watched her leave, just like Dad had watched Roman leave all those years ago.

The flashing police lights turned off, and when Roman dragged his gaze from the snowy woods where Mila had disappeared, Rhett was staring in the same direction with pure fury in his eyes. Something dark and ugly churned in his gut at Rhett glaring after

Mila like that, but it also gave him the very beginnings of an idea.

His brother, Gentry, wanted to break apart the Bone-Ripper Pack just like he did the wild wolves he'd been trained to hunt, but that wouldn't work. Gentry was forgetting one essential thing—the Bone-Rippers weren't wild wolves.

Roman gave Rhett a remorseless smile. He was going to hunt the pack his own way, by digging into the weakest member, and then work his way through the ranks, dropping little grenades until he reached the very top.

Roman was going to annihilate Rhett for all he'd done to his Dad, to this town, to Blaire, and to that hunter in the body bag.

But first, he needed to turn Mila against her alpha.

TWO

Mila scribbled another circle onto a notepad full of them and blew her bangs out of her face. They settled right back down in front of her eyes, though. She needed a haircut, but then, it was so nice to hide from Rhett. Her alpha liked to look right in her eyes as if he was trying to see into her soul, and as silly as it sounded, the bangs provided a little shield, so she let them grow.

The door opened, and she looked up hopefully for a customer, but nope, it was just Tim who owned this place now. Business was at a standstill since Rhett had decided to chase the humans from the bar. It made shifts at the Four Horsemen tedious at best.

"Trouble's comin'," Tim murmured, a storm in his

eyes.

"Rhett?" she asked in a higher pitch than she'd intended. She was supposed to have a few more hours before he showed up here tonight.

Tim walked right past the bar, his bushy, gray brows lowered in thought, as though he hadn't heard her.

The door swung open, and in with the snowflakes blew Roman Striker. Mila swallowed a yelp as the door banked against the wall.

He wore a thin white T-shirt over dark jeans with holes at the knees. Dark tendrils of ink marked up both arms. He hadn't had any tattoos when he'd left here at seventeen. He hadn't worn a thick beard either. His piercing blue eyes were still the same, but that was about it. Roman looked like a man now. It was such a strange sensation comparing the man who stood in the doorway, eyes locked on her, with the boy she used to know. With the boy she had secretly crushed on from afar.

Now he was taller, layered with muscle, covered in tattoos, and from the circular shapes pressing against the threadbare material of his shirt, he had his nipples pierced, too. Roman dropped his chin to his chest, eyes holding hers while a slow, sensual smile stretched his lips. "You look different, too."

Mila clutched the pad of doodles to her chest and kept the shocked gasp squarely in her throat. "I-I wasn't checking you out."

"Bullshit, but I don't mind." He pulled off a navy winter hat and ran his hand through his blond hair roughly. It somehow made him look sexier instead of slobby.

Roman closed the door and strode over to the to-go station she was sitting behind, his boots unlaced, the tongue of his shoes flopping with each deliberate step. He was graceful, but much louder than she remembered. Maybe that came with the size. She was like a mouse—quiet, striving for invisibility, always careful with her movements.

"What are you doing here?" she murmured low as he made his way behind the bar. "If Rhett catches you in here—"

"What? He'll kill me like he did that hunter?"

"Shhh," she hissed, looking around. "He didn't kill him."

Roman was talking about things he didn't understand.

Stupid boy.

Roman arched his eyebrow and gave her a dead-eyed look. Well, Rhett *probably* didn't kill the hunter. She didn't really know. Rhett was capable of awful things.

Roman squared up to her and slid his hands onto her waist.

"Wh-what are you doing?"

"Seducing you."

"Stop!" Mila swatted his hand, but he was backing her slowly to the wall with a wicked grin on his lips. "I'm not playing games with you, Roman. Whatever you're here for, spill it and let me be." She had enough problems without Rhett seeing Roman with his hands on her. God, she couldn't even imagine her alpha's reaction. He *hated* the Striker brothers.

"I have a business proposition," Roman murmured, trapping her into a corner out of view of the door. He smelled like toothpaste and cologne—the good stuff. It was making her dizzy.

"What?"

"Focus, Mila."

She was. She was focused on the way his lips formed her name. He sure wore a beard well.

Roman leaned forward, his smile widening as he did. His lips were right by her ear when something brushed her hand, and he said, "There's no way you're making enough here to cover your bills. This place is a pit." He held a folded piece of paper against her palm. "Let me guess, your alpha chased all the paying customers out. Not shocking. Rhett is shit at leadership. You know he'll split this town and throw suspicion on the pack in a year tops."

Actually, he'd managed that in the first week of being alpha, but Roman didn't need to know that.

"Or has he already done that, I wonder?" Roman asked. "Has he, Mila?"

"Y-yes." *Shit. Stop talking.*

"Good girl."

His body was so warm against hers now. She normally would've felt trapped about now, wanting to curl up in a ball and disappear, but something was happening to her body. She was tingling, and fire was flowing through her veins from where he held her hand up her arm and into her chest. That felt nice, but after a couple of seconds, another sensation took over. Roman was too dominant and way too close, and her lungs were slowly freezing in her ribcage.

Roman's nostrils flared as he scented the air. "Still a little chicken."

Mila hated the acrid scent of her fear, but that was the curse of the submissive wolf that dwelled within her. She was in a constant state of fear—especially in Rangeley.

Roman backed off a few paces, and that worked enough for her to drag a shallow breath in. She looked down at the paper he'd left in her hand. There was a drawing of a dick on it. It had a frowney face on the balls.

"Why did you give me a cartoon penis?" she asked.

"What?" Roman frowned at the paper and then chuckled an amused sound. "Oh yeah, I was drawing Asher. Open it up. It's a present."

Mila unfolded the worn paper carefully. It was a *Now Hiring* announcement for Winter's Edge, the rival bar in town. The one Roman's father had run before he'd been silenced by Rhett. She checked the door again real quick and then looked around for Tim, but she and Roman were alone. She lowered her voice to a whisper. "Roman, what are you doing?" She held up the paper. "This can't happen. I can't go work at your bar!"

"Why not?" Roman wore a cocky grin as he leaned back against the counter. She could see the perfect indentations of his abs right through his shirt.

Focus.

"You keep looking at my dick."

"I'm not! I don't. It's your"—she waved her hand at his stomach—"freaking...twenty pack. Do you work out all the time now? I mean...is a million crunches a day really necessary?" *Stop talking.*

"You look mad. Or flustered. Am I flustering you, Little Chicken?"

"Stop calling me that. We aren't kids anymore, Roman. There is a hundred years and a canyon between now and where we used to be. You can't just come back in here looking like...that...and think you can pick up where we left off."

"Where did we leave off?" he asked innocently.

Games. Now she remembered it all so clearly. Roman loved playing games. He loved toying with people, and apparently he had his sights set on her tonight. Mila crumpled up the paper and chucked it at him. When it bounced off his chest, he caught it without even looking down. Of course he did. He was probably great with his hands.

Stupid boy.

Mila dug deep and found enough bravery to jam her finger at the front door. "Leave."

"I'll pay you double what you make here, and you don't have to share your tips with the other servers."

"Roman," she pleaded, "you're going to get me hurt."

The smile fell from his face, and he stood up straighter, taller. Something terrifying flashed in the melted-gold color of his eyes. He clenched his jaw once and smelled of fury for just an instant before he huffed a breath and softened his face again. One side of his mouth turned up in a crooked smile that probably got him a lot of blow jobs. "No one will hurt you, Chicken." Roman turned and strode toward the door, tugging on his winter hat as he went. "Interviews are at nine o'clock tomorrow morning," he called over his shoulder without turning around. At the door, he pulled it open and turned that crooked grin on her once again. "You're my first choice."

He stayed locked on her gaze for a moment more, then ducked his chin and disappeared out into the windy parking lot. When the door slammed closed behind him, Mila jumped at the bang.

You're my first choice. She had longed for those words from him through school. Longed for him to notice her, but he liked other girls. He liked the dominant girls—the ones who were loud and fun and stayed the center of attention. And now, eight years later, he'd finally uttered the words her heart had wanted so badly to belong to her.

But she was a game to him.

Mila could see it in his smirk and his dancing eyes. Roman had never learned how to be serious—not really. And now he was tempting her to go against Rhett, tempting her to put herself in danger just so he could play?

That hurt.

Stupid boy.

THREE

She shouldn't be here.

Mila gripped the steering wheel of her Jetta and blew out a frozen breath. The car hadn't even gotten the chance to warm up before she was sitting in the parking lot of Winter's Edge. Memories flooded her. Playing with Asher, Gentry, and Roman in the woods behind the bar while the old Striker pack held meetings inside. Gentry locking her and Roman in the freezer once, calling it Seven Minutes in Heaven. There had been no kissing, though. Mostly Roman had beaten on the door and yelled at his brother while Mila had sat huddled in the corner, scared of Roman's already dominant wolf, even at twelve years old. She remembered countless dinners with the pack at Hunter Cove Inn just through the woods. Changing with the Striker brothers. Howling like she was one of them. Roman's face when he and Asher were kicked out of the pack. That had been one of the worst meetings she'd ever been to. The devastation on his face would haunt her soul forever.

She'd practically grown up here. How many life lessons had been taught by her elders right here, in Winter's Edge.

She still couldn't believe Noah Striker was dead. If the Striker brothers knew what really happened to their father, they would call the Bone-Rippers to war. They wouldn't understand how messed up everything had gotten. But if she was in their position, and it was her dad who had to be put down, she would want her pound of flesh, too.

She shouldn't be here.

She should be back in bed, enjoying her morning off, sleeping in, making pancakes, or reading the newspaper, doing literally anything other than sitting in the parking lot of Winter's Edge, wishing everything had turned out differently.

The side entrance door swung open, and out ran Blaire Hayward, redheaded mate of Gentry and brand new wolf. Mila didn't know how to feel about her yet. She was probably a nice person, but truth be told, Mila was envious of how easy her life was. She'd landed Gentry, dominant protector. Not only that, but her wolf felt much more dominant whenever she was around her. She could probably defend herself just fine, while Mila was at everyone's mercy. And she got to live here, in beautiful Hunter Cove, and work for some publisher with some fancy job she got to do from home. She and Gentry would have a dozen pups and live happily ever after, while Mila was bound to a life of nothingness in the Bone-Ripper Pack.

Blaire was running now. No. Mila sat forward and tracked her movement through the woods. She was stumbling.

Mila shoved the car door open and made her way silently across the frozen parking lot. The scent of blood filled her nose and made her hesitate on the edge of the woods. Tiny, red flecks dotted the white snow.

Blaire was hurt.

Mila cast a quick glance behind her at Winter's Edge and then made her way through the forest, following the blood trail Blair had left in her wake.

Perhaps the lucky wolf had cut herself with a knife in the kitchen. But when she heard the sobbing and smelled that inky, heavy black magic that was so familiar, she knew Blaire was in bad trouble.

She should leave. This was none of Mila's business, but Blaire was muttering something now, over and over. "Please, please, please." Who was she begging? The wind? The woods? Mila?

She had to have known she was there. Her wolf would sense her, but Blaire sat on her knees in the snow, her back to Mila, her shoulders shaking with her body-wracking sobs.

"Blaire?" Mila asked, stepping carefully over a log.

Blaire gasped and twisted around. Her nose was streaming blood and dripping down her chin, and her glowing green eyes were so scared. "Don't tell him. Please don't tell him."

Mila approached carefully as Blaire doubled into herself and groaned, then straightened again.

"What's wrong with you?"

"I don't know. I can't Change. I try and try, I feel her right there, but I keep getting these nose bleeds and these headaches. Ooooh," she groaned as she fell onto the snow and curled into herself. Blaire hugged her knees as tears streamed down her face.

The stink of black magic was so thick it was choking Mila, but now it made horrifying sense how Blaire had survived. "Did the witch raise your wolf?"

"Yes," Blaire whispered brokenly.

"Jesus," Mila murmured, kneeling beside her.

"Jesus had nothing to do with what happened to me. I know your scent. You were there. You helped kill me."

"No, I was there as a witness, but I didn't help in the hunt."

"It's getting worse," Blaire murmured, her entire body trembling. "If I can't Change, something bad will happen, won't it?"

No point in lying. Changes were crucial. There had to be a balance between the wolf and the human side, or one would kill the other. And if one died, they both died.

Blaire looked so pale and frightened against the red-splattered snow. Her freckles were stark against her cheeks, and her tears were freezing at the corners of her eyes. "Gentry is bound to me."

"Oh, my gosh," Mila murmured, lifting Blaire's shoulders until her head was in her lap. "That's why you don't want to tell him? You don't want him to know he'll..."

"You can say it."

He'll die, too. Mila couldn't force the words up her throat. The White Wolf of Winter's Edge wasn't as privileged as Mila had assumed. Blaire was bound by black magic into a life she hadn't chosen, just like her.

Mila hated Odine. Clearly she'd ruined yet another life. Two, if Blaire and Gentry were really bound. Werewolves died with their bound mates.

Blaire had stopped crying, and the smell of pain and black magic dissipated as Mila stroked her fiery locks away from her face.

"I'm sorry," Blaire said suddenly, sitting up. "I panicked, but I'm okay now."

Mila would have had an easier time believing her if Blaire didn't still have blood on her face. Gentry's mate began scrubbing her face with snow so Mila stood up and dusted off her jeans. "You should tell him."

"He's got so much on his plate right now with settling the inn and re-opening Winter's Edge. I don't want to worry him more. I'll figure it out. I'm just new and bad at Changes, but I'll learn."

Mila didn't know how it worked for Turned wolves—not many humans survived the bite—but she was pretty sure it shouldn't be this hard for Blaire to call her wolf. "Come on, I'll walk you back to the bar."

"Okay," Blaire said quietly as she wiped her face on the sleeve of her black sweater.

"Look, Gentry will smell the blood on you." Mila shrugged one shoulder up. "You'll have to hide that stuff better. And maybe talk to the witch about what she did to your wolf."

Blaire's gaze flicked to Mila and then away into the woods as she began walking back toward Winter's Edge. "If you were me, would you ask Odine for help?"

A moment of memory from the night Odine had bound Mila to Rangeley was enough to warrant a quick response. "Hell no."

Blaire gave a sad smile. "I'll figure it out on my own." Her voice held a false note to it, though, as if she didn't really believe that herself.

Roman stood leaned against the building near the side entrance when Mila came out of the tree line.

Blaire gave her a little wave and tromped around

the building, but Roman was watching the redhead with narrowed eyes. He scented the air, his nostrils flaring slightly as he lifted his chin. "Is she okay?" he asked Mila.

Mila couldn't lie to a werewolf, so she shrugged and made a beeline for the parking lot.

"Where are you going?" Roman asked, trailing her.

"Home."

"Why?"

"Because I shouldn't be here."

"But you are here. You got up early and put on those cute fucking clothes, that cute fucking scarf, and that pink, little hat. Even matched your lip gloss to it, didn't you? For me?"

"Roman, the world doesn't revolve around you."

He drew up in front of her and planted his feet, stopping her in her tracks. "You're different than before. You feel different. Still a chicken but…more."

"Games, Roman. I still don't play them."

"Yet you're here," he said lifting his chin higher. The man was standing so close she could feel his body warmth through her layers. He'd always run hotter than any person she'd ever met. She'd forgotten about that. Hot Roman, she used to call him in her diary. Hot as a Roman candle.

"Five minutes. Come on," he urged. "There are three people in there applying for jobs, and they are all boring as hell." His lip snarled up with mischief. "If I'm going to work that bar, I want someone fun to play with."

Irritated, she dared a quick look to his eyes before she ducked her gaze again. Her wolf was reacting strangely to Roman's. Cowering, but she wanted to be closer. It was as if she couldn't make up her mind, and it was putting Mila in an uncomfortable in-between state of fight *and* flight. "So you aren't leaving then?"

"Oh, I'll leave as soon as I'm able, Chicken. Doesn't mean we can't have a little fun while I'm in town."

Mila shook her head, angry at how much his flippant talk about leaving again hurt her. She knew better than to get attached to a Striker. Runners, the lot of them. That had been the point of her warning him, right? To chase him off? To save him from Rhett's wrath? To save him from the teeth of the Bone-Rippers? So why was she angry that he had admitted he was leaving soon?

Because you're broken.

She huffed a sharp breath and sidestepped around him. "Good luck hiring for Winter's Edge. You'll have this place crawling with humans in no time."

"Whoo, you sounded bitter just then. Did you hear yourself? Since when did it become us and them, hmm? Humans and wolves."

"You've been gone a long time, Roman. Things are different in this town now. It's not like the outside world anymore. It's best to stay separate." She gave a glance to the front door. Blaire was inside that building scrubbing the rest of the blood from her face in the bathroom. She'd been human, and healthy, and now look. Mixing got people killed, both wolves and humans.

"I'll drive," Roman said, hooking an arm around her waist and steering her away from her black Jetta toward a silver Jeep Wrangler. It was a monster, big tires, black-out rims, mud flaps, cable hooks on the front for hauling people out of ditches, the works. Sharp icicles that hung from the front end looked like teeth.

"Drive us where? I thought you had interviews."

"Asher can handle them. He loves social interaction." Roman laughed at his own joke, and despite herself, Mila cracked a grin. The oldest Striker brother had never loved people. "There's this breakfast place I want to try. Jack's. You heard of it?" Roman asked, bumping her shoulder.

She locked her legs against any forward motion and frowned at his back as he kept walking. "What are you doing?"

"Taking a stroll down memory lane," he uttered, turning slowly. He wasn't smiling anymore, and his eyes flashed with something she didn't understand.

"I figured you didn't remember that morning."

Roman's eyes tightened, and a muscle twitched in his jaw. "How could I forget something like that?"

Mila crossed her arms over her chest and shook her head, stared off into the woods. She'd found Roman in the woods right after he'd turned seventeen. He'd been kicked out of the pack and had gotten into the whiskey at Winter's Edge.

And when she closed her eyes, she was transported right back to that moment.

"Roman?"

ROMAN

"Don't come any closer, Mila. I'm not okay."

Roman was snarling, and it scared her, but he was her friend. He wouldn't hurt her. Still, the closer she got to the boy sitting in the snow with his back to her, the heavier the pressure on her shoulders. Roman was a monster who had been very good at hiding. With a whimper, she went down to her knees and crawled closer. "I'm sorry, Roman."

Roman turned slowly and looked at her, his eyes the color of saturated sunlight, his face twisted into something terrifying. He smelled like liquor, and there was an empty bottle toppled over in the snow. "Can you see them, Mila?"

"See what?" she rasped out, face averted, neck exposed to the animal that was snarling in Roman's throat.

"The ghosts. They're always here. Some darkness inside of me draws them. They can see my shadows. I am home to them."

"I-I don't understand."

"Your mom says she misses you."

Fury blasted through her. "Don't talk like that."

"Everyone thinks the people of this town get buried and they find rest. Not here, though, Mila," Roman

slurred. "Maybe it's best my dad kicked me out of the pack." The anger in his voice lashed across her skin like the end of a whip.

"He was wrong, Roman. I won't join unless he lets you back in. I won't pledge."

"You don't have a choice. You're submissive. Your life was laid out the moment your wolf came out cowered. Lucky."

Mila's eyes burned, and she blinked hard. "You shouldn't have said that about my mom. You did it to hurt me."

Roman blurred to her so fast she gasped. He hugged her tight, on his knees in the snow, crushing her to him, rocking gently. Her initial instinct was to push away from the monster and bolt, but Roman was stroking her hair gently, over and over, petting her, calming her. "You'll pledge to the Striker Pack, and you'll stay safe. Do you understand? I hate my dad, but he can keep a submissive safe."

"And you'll be here, too," she squeaked out, gripping his shirt. "You'll be a part of this town, just not in the pack. You can keep me safe, too. You're my friend. I'll keep you safe back."

Roman swallowed audibly. "Sure, Mila."

And then he'd picked her up like she was a child and carried her to her car. It was an old Buick her dad had just given her for her sixteenth birthday. He tucked her behind the wheel and buckled her in, and then he climbed in the passenger's seat and told her, "I'm not ready for tonight to be over. Not ready to sleep. Not ready to say goodnight to you, Chicken."

"Where do you want to go?"

"Jack's."

Mila wanted to cry at the memory. He'd left the next day without a goodbye, but she'd had that night, eating pancakes at the all-night diner with the boy she'd liked for so long. She'd thought they were bonding and he was starting to like her, but Roman had been silently saying his goodbye to her instead, while she'd been unaware, laughing at all his jokes and feeling happy.

"Do you still see dead people?" she asked, feeling nauseous by how real and unexpected that memory had been.

Roman snorted and made his way toward the jeep. "Nobody sees dead people, Mila. I was just drunk that night."

But his voice sounded strange, with a note of falseness, and the smile in his eyes had dimmed as he stood holding her door open. While she stared at him, his gaze flicked twice to something in the woods behind her, but when she turned, nothing was there.

And then Roman was grinning when she looked at him again.

More games.

Mila rolled her eyes and muttered, "Fine. Jack's, but only because I skipped breakfast."

FOUR

Roman scrubbed his hand down his beard and leaned back for the waitress to set the two giant orders of pancakes in front of him. He was having trouble taking his eyes off Mila. When she'd removed her hat and matching pink scarf, her dark bangs had flopped forward in front of her smoky, champagne-colored eyes. She'd grown up to be a fucking ten. Curves just right on her little body, tight ass, perky tits she'd shoved into a push-up bra. He could see the very edge of that bra, nude lace, peeking up out of her white V-neck sweater. A gentleman would've told her she was showing bra, but he was no gentleman. So here he sat like the total fuckin' perv he was, sneaking peeks at that little strip of lace and thanking his lucky stars the table hid his boner.

He needed to cut this shit out. This was the game. This was the hunt. He was supposed to dig into Mila and piss off Rhett, scatter the others, cause reactions, push boundaries. But with every second he was spending with her, he remembered how much he'd liked her when they were kids. He'd stayed in the friend zone, but not because he didn't want to suck face with her up at Lookout Point. He'd stayed away because she was too fragile, too submissive, too sweet, and too good for him. He'd always been one spark from igniting, and would've burned up Mila right along with him.

While Mila poured syrup over her waffles, he imagined her pouring it onto him and licking it off with that cute little mouth of hers. He couldn't even remember the last time he was this turned on. Roman cleared his throat. "Does Nelda still run that logging crew?"

"She oversees it, but Farris is running it now."

Fuck, Farris would be a harder sell.

"Why?" Mila asked suddenly, looking up at him with narrowed eyes. Wolf eyes. God, he loved that wild color on her face. She was so good. Roman wanted to corrupt her and release that bad wolf he knew was buried in her somewhere. *Buried...in her.* Fuuuuuck, he wanted to take her out to the back of his jeep and lose his mind, strip her down, and push into her until she was screaming his name.

Mila was staring at him like he'd already lost that sanity. What had she asked him? Oh yeah, why was he asking about Nelda's logging crew. "I was thinking about asking for a job."

"I thought you had a job."

The lace was the exact same shade as her skin. "Hmmm? Oh, right, the bar. Extra income."

"You've been around humans too long," she murmured so quietly no one would hear but him. "Your lies work with them. Not on me."

Oh yeah, crap. "Fine, I want a pack job so I can stir the shit in the Bone-Rippers."

"Is that what you're doing here with me?" she asked carefully, her eyes downcast as she cut her waffle into perfect squares.

"I don't know yet." She wouldn't find a lie in that because now he was confused about why he'd asked her to Jack's, of all places in this town. It was like he'd wanted her to remember that hug in the woods. Had it meant as much to her as it had to him? All he knew was that when he'd held Mila, the ghosts in the woods had scattered, and he'd found peace for a few minutes.

"Roman, why are you here?" she asked softly, lifting those pretty eyes to him. He wanted to see all of them, wanted to brush her bangs out of her face, smooth them back, see if her skin was as soft as it looked. See if *she* was as soft as she looked...

"I came to be with my brothers when my dad's ashes were spread."

Sympathy pooled in her eyes. "Did you already scatter his ashes over the river?"

"Uuuum, no. Asherhole dumped them right behind Winter's Edge while me and Gentry were trying to stop him, and we all got covered in Dad. It was fucking gross." And now Dad's ghost wouldn't leave him alone. That probably had something to do with it, which was why Roman currently hated Asher the most out of his brothers right now.

Mila hid a smile, but not well enough.

"It's not funny. I got ashes in my mouth."

She snorted and pursed her lips harder as her eyes got round like dinner plates. And now a cute pink color was staining her cheeks. Roman liked making people laugh in general, but Mila was serious, submissive, and she'd always presented him with a challenge. She didn't give smiles as easily as other people, but she was giving him one now. A feeling of triumph slowly unfurled in his chest.

"Your dad would be so disappointed in the three of you," she teased. "All he ever talked about was fishing on that damn river."

"Please, he would be disappointed in Asher, not me and Gentry. Gentry was his favorite son, and he never gave two shits about me. No feelings, no disappointment. But Asher broke the urn on a tree. I'm pretty sure we were supposed to...I don't know...keep that as a memento or something."

"Your dad cared about you," Mila said, her pretty face scrunching up in a frown. "Noah talked about all three of you, all the time. There wasn't a single pack meeting where you three weren't brought up. Not just Gentry, not just Asher. He always talked about how you worked your way up a construction crew faster than anyone he'd ever heard of, and how you were always so good at fixing anything."

Roman laughed unsurely. "You're making this

up."

"No, I'm not." She gave a quick shrug. "He even had your pictures hanging in Winter's Edge until…"

Roman narrowed his eyes. "Until what?"

Mila froze, her eyes big like a deer in headlights. The smell of her fear ripped a snarl out of his throat. The aggression wasn't directed at her. Instead, it was a protective instinct to murder whatever had scared her. But at the sound in his throat, she whimpered and shrank back into her seat. Roman then realized what had scared her…was him.

She knew things. She knew about the mysteries he and his brothers had been trying to unravel since the day they had come back into town, but Mila had a loyalty problem. She was pledged to the Bone-Rippers, and apparently bound by black magic to Rangeley. Roman was an outsider, one she didn't trust. But he wanted to change that. And not just because he wanted to fuck with the pack anymore. It genuinely bothered him that Mila still couldn't relax around him. It wasn't like they'd just met. They'd grown up together. He wanted her trust. Wanted to earn it, wanted her to give it.

Dad was standing across the bar. He wasn't being

normal ghost Dad either. He was standing half in the wall, right under a pair of deer antlers, staring...still staring. He'd kept pictures of Roman in Winter's Edge. *Did you, Dad? Did you secretly care?*

Mila slid her legs forward under the table and rested her ankles against his. Shocked, he jerked his attention to her, but she didn't look scared anymore. Her eyes were soft. He wished he could say something witty and make her smile again. Her legs felt good against his. It had been a long time since someone touched him on purpose.

"Who's there, Roman?" Mila asked.

Roman dragged his gaze back to the wall, but there was no ghost there anymore. "No one," he murmured. "No one but you."

Mila rubbed her ankle against him gently, and before he could stop himself, he reached under the table and gripped her under her knee. So warm. So fragile. She was small, and he could snap her leg without much effort, but she didn't jerk away. Instead, as he rubbed his thumb along the seam of her jeans, she rolled her eyes closed and released a quiet, shaky breath. So fucking beautiful.

"Mila," Rhett barked out from the door.

She instantly froze like a statue, every muscle in her leg tense, and the scent of her fear was all Roman could smell. The reaction of her body made Roman want to rip Rhett's throat out. He released her knee slowly and leaned back on the bench seat, glaring at the alpha of the Bone-Rippers. Another black mark against Rhett, another reason Roman wanted to pull his intestines through his mouth hole.

Mila didn't say a word but pushed out of the bench seat, eyes downcast, and slunk over to Rhett. His face was red with fury, and he pulled her against his side hard. Roman snarled, but Mila gave him a warning glance. Right…there were humans in here.

"Stay away from my girl, Striker," Rhett said in a low, gravelly voice. His eyes were too bright. If anyone was going to get them busted in Jack's, it was going to be Rhett.

His girl? Mila was huddled into his side, sure, but her expression was a mixture of terror and disgust.

"You forgot your purse, Chicken," Roman murmured. *Come back to me.*

Mila hunched into herself even deeper and shrugged out from under Rhett's arm. She walked in jerky steps back to the table, leaned over the seat, then grabbed her purse and jacket. "Look in the freezer of Winter's Edge. I saved the pictures right before we closed the bar," Mila said on a breath. Her face was pale as a sheet as she stood with her things. "Goodbye, Roman," she said at normal volume. Mila looked as if she'd never curved her lips into a grin her whole life.

"For good," Rhett called. "Mila, I forbid you to talk to him or any of the Strikers again." Power wafted through his words, and Mila's eyes rimmed with tears. She looked sick as the power of the order pushed her forward gently, then rocked her back. She hadn't taken her eyes from Roman's, and now they lightened even more. There was no snarl or fight from her wolf. Just acceptance. Roman had always thought her lucky to be submissive, to have her life planned out, to have a wolf that would demand protection from the males around her.

All this time he'd been wrong.

"Come here," Rhett demanded.

And Mila did. She turned and made her way right back under his arm, where she probably stayed when he wanted to manipulate her. Rhett kissed her hard. It was a second, and then it was done, but his eyes had stayed on Roman. When he jerked her back by the neck of her shirt, he was smiling and Mila's lip was bleeding.

Roman wanted to stand up and put himself between her and Rhett. He wanted to drag the alpha out to the parking lot and beat his ass into a puddle of nothing. Into a stain in the snow.

Roman had given Mila smiles, and that asshole had stolen them away.

FIVE

No one but you. You're my first choice.

Oh, Roman was good. Much smoother than he'd been as a boy, and now she felt like she was in trouble, especially with the order Rhett had just thrown down in the doorway of Jack's. He wasn't careful. He never had been. He'd pulled that crap right there in front of six tables of humans.

That order had hurt so bad to accept. But even now, as she thought of sneaking to Winter's Edge to see Roman again, her stomach curdled with nausea. It would get worse if she tried to disobey her alpha.

Rhett was gripping her arm too tight as he dragged her through the parking lot of Jack's. He felt terrifyingly heavy right now. So heavy she couldn't drag the cold air into her lungs, or even catch her breath enough to tell him she didn't want to get in his car with him.

He shoved her into the passenger's seat of his truck and slammed the door so hard the vehicle rocked up on two wheels. Frantically, she looked around to see if anyone had seen his show of strength. Rhett was wearing his police uniform, and the truck was a black and white with lights on the roof. He was on duty, so why was he here messing with her?

Rhett slid behind the wheel and slammed his own door, then roared, his breath freezing in front of him like a dragon blowing smoke.

"H-how did you know where I was?" she asked in a mouse voice.

"Because you're mine!" he yelled as he jammed the key in the ignition. "I can feel you. I can feel when you're betraying me. Betraying the pack. I can feel when you're being a little whore." He skidded out of the icy parking lot and onto Main Street. "I'm taking you out tonight."

"Out in the woods?" she asked, terrified.

"I want to pretty fuckin' bad right now, Mila! I

want to fuckin'—" He wrapped his hand around her throat and squeezed, and then he shook her as he blasted down Main. "Seeing you with him makes me want to punish you, Mila," he said in a softer voice, releasing her neck. "It makes me want to give into my urges. Do you understand?"

No, she didn't understand. What urges? Sex? Murder? Mila was too terrified to ask. Rhett's wolf had always been broken.

"I hate when you kiss me like that," she whispered.

"I know." He tossed her an evil smile. "That's why I like doing it so much. Any other female in my pack would revel in the attention, but not you. When I fuck you, you'll make it a challenge for me. You'll scream. You'll get me off because you'll fight it. I'm going to take you out so we can say the courting is done. Buy you a fucking hamburger or something, get through technicalities, and then I will call a Pack meeting tomorrow. I will announce my choice in alpha female. You don't belong to Roman, or to anyone else, Mila." He flashed her a fiery glance. "I own you. You're my bitch, you understand?"

"I don't want to be alpha female," she forced past

her tightening vocal chords. "You don't own—"

"Bullshit, I don't!" he yelled, slamming his fist against the steering wheel. He was driving too fast, scaring her even more. "Since the day you pledged to me, I knew I would have you."

"But you sleep with Amanda and Ashley."

"And I'll continue sleeping with them. It's in my nature. But if you so much as glance at Roman Striker ever again, I'll kill you both, and I'll be brutal about it. I don't share well."

"No."

Rhett slammed on the brakes and skidded his truck sideways, right on the edge of town. "What did you just say?"

Mila pressed her body against the door and wished she could move enough to roll down the window, just to give herself some relief from his anger and his dominance. Just so she could breath and clear her head enough to be strong. "I said no," she whispered. "I don't want you. I don't want alpha female."

Rhett blasted a furious laugh. "Mila, your first mistake is in thinking I give a shit what you want. Your wants don't count, *Chicken*."

She shook her head hard, pissed he was using Roman's nickname to hurt her. She *hated* Rhett. Always had, always would.

"You'll sit on the throne I give you, and you'll spread your legs when I demand it, give me the pups I want, and you'll be at my back as I bring this town around to our ways." He stomped his boot on the floorboard hard and yelled, "Am I fucking clear, Mila?"

A honk sounded. Someone in a black Mazda was trying to get Rhett's attention from his side of the truck. He sighed a snarl and then plastered on a smile before rolling down the window.

This was her chance. Mila shoved open the door. Rhett's hand went immediately to her sleeve, but she wrenched her arm away from him. *Riiiip*. He was left with shredded fabric and her jacket and purse as Mila bolted from his truck.

"Mila!" he yelled.

She plugged her ears, hoping to hell that would help as she bolted for the snowy tree line. *Please don't give a command to go back to him!* If he did, her wolf would betray her. She always did.

Mila sprinted into the trees, her boots crunching

in the ankle-deep snow, her breath heaving in her chest, the frozen fog blurring her vision. Limbs whipped at her face and arms as she ran. Inside of her, the wolf writhed and scratched to escape her skin. Mila couldn't allow it. She would go back to him. She would go back to the pack. She would go back thinking she was safe with their alpha, but her wolf had never understood safety.

Subservience had cast a fog over her instincts, and now she walked a fine line between life and death.

Her tears were cold on her cheeks. Through the woods, movement flashed. Gray fur. God, Rhett was hunting her. A sob wrenched from her as she pushed her legs harder. *Don't Change. Not even if he howls. Not even if he calls you.*

The inky tendrils of black magic wafted over her skin in the same second all the whispering started. No, no, no. Something bad must've happened in these woods, but Mila couldn't stop running or Rhett would catch her. Catch her like a bunny. Like prey. She didn't want to be prey anymore.

Movement flashed on her other side. It was a charcoal gray wolf, one of the biggest she'd ever seen.

Gentry. In front of her, a monster pitch-black wolf bolted through the trees. Pumping her legs, she checked her right side again, but the gray fur didn't belong to Rhett. It was Roman's wolf. Gray and brown with lighter points. Massive. Monster. Gold eyes, but he wasn't looking at her. He was looking straight ahead. Not hunting her. Running with her.

Wait...she'd done this before.

Mila skidded to a stop in the snow. Her hands flickered to mottled gray wolf paws, then back and forth again. Chugging breath, she looked up at the circling Striker brothers. Friends. But Asher started melting away, not disappearing, but his skin liquefied and slid onto the snow in strips. He looked like a zombie wolf for a moment before he fell into a pile of bones. Gentry did the same. "No!" she screamed as Roman sat in the snow right next to her. He trapped her in his gaze before his skin, too, began to melt away. Mila fell to her knees as he turned into a pile of nothing. Behind him, the same color as Roman's bones, the White Wolf of Winter's Edge stood, staring at Mila with glowing green eyes.

You still have me. Still have me. Me. You have me.
The words tumbled over and over in Mila's head. She

grabbed her hair and shook herself hard. This wasn't real. *Wake up!*

The stink of black magic made her retch in the snow, but when she looked up again, the white wolf was gone, and Blaire sat there on her knees instead.

"Mila?" she asked, wiping her bloody nose.

"What's happening?"

Blaire shook her head and let off a frightened sound in her throat. "I don't know," she whispered. "I don't know how I got here. My wolf won't come out. Mila, I'm scared."

Bring her to me. Odine stood near a towering pine tree. *Mila, bring her to me.*

Then Odine disappeared in a puff of dark smoke.

Black magic did this to the woods. Until it dissipated, horrors would live here. Mila ran her hand over the snow where Roman's bones had been just to convince herself he was still okay. Blaire was real, though. Maybe the bad magic was coming from her.

"What do you see?" Mila asked her.

Blaire looked around the woods with wide green eyes, her red hair lifting in the stiff wind. "Nothing."

Shit. Blaire was in deep if she couldn't even tell

the effects of the magic that was pulsing from her body. Mila stood and made her way to the woman, but hesitated touching her because she didn't feel right. She felt dangerous.

Mila knelt and scooped her up, then carried her through the woods toward Hunter Cove. She followed Blaire's tracks until she could see the smoke from the chimney of the inn. And then Roman was there, standing on the tree line, leaned against a spruce, his arms crossed over his chest like he'd been waiting for her.

Mila was happy to see him. Relieved, but her stomach hurt worse every step she took toward him. Defying Rhett's order was making her sick.

She stumbled with Blaire in her arms, but he blurred to her and took the burden of the weight from Mila.

"How did you know I was here?" she asked shakily, wrapping her arms around her stomach to keep herself from shredding apart.

"Best if I don't say." He turned with Blaire in his arms and made his way toward his Jeep.

"W-where are you going?"

"Psychodine's."

She would've laughed at his unexpected nickname if all of this wasn't so seriously un-funny. "Roman, I don't think that's a good idea. She's been summoning Blaire—"

"Blaire's really sick, Mila. Can't you smell it? She and Gentry have a few days left at most. He hasn't woken up all day. It's the witch or death, and I just got my brother back. This is your pack's fault. This is your alpha's fault. You want to help fix this? Get in the Jeep."

"I can't."

"You can," he called over his shoulder.

"No, you don't understand. I am under an order to stay away from you!"

Roman loaded Blair into the back of his Jeep and then turned a furious gaze on Mila. "Fight it."

And she wanted to. She wanted to find her inner badass and cut her heart from the pack. She wanted to take a knife to the ropes that tethered her to Rhett. She wanted to be strong like Roman. But her stomach already hurt so bad, and she felt so weak she couldn't imagine riding in a car with Roman right now. "I'm sorry," she murmured.

Roman's lips twitched into a sad smile that didn't

reach his eyes. "Me, too."

And then he got into his Jeep, shut the door, and pulled away.

SIX

Roman rubbed the chills from his arms and shook his head for the tenth time since he'd sat his butt on the bottom step of Odine's cabin. Whatever she was doing inside had sucked the warmth from him. He'd rarely been cold in his life, but she was draining him. He felt like shit, and the longer he sat here, the worse it got.

"She needs it," Asher murmured as Roman stood to go pace the yard. "Don't burn energy right now."

When Roman looked up to the top step of the porch, Asher looked like death warmed over and was slumped against the railing.

"Son of a fucknugget," Roman gritted out. "Is she gonna kill us all?"

"She won't kill us."

"Yeah, and how do you know that?"

Asher didn't answer, and Roman hated him a little more for all his damned secrets. Always defending the black witch, and for what?

"Because she saved Blaire once, asshole. She didn't have to, and it hurt her to do it, but she did it anyway. And if you think she isn't draining herself in there trying to bring back Blaire and Gentry, you're wrong. She's shaving years off her life for them."

"You reading minds now, Asher? Is that what dancing with the devil earns you? Stay out of my head." Roman concentrated really hard on a cartoon dick dancing the Macarena, but Asher didn't react. Maybe he was full of bullshit like everyone else in Roman's life. "What kind of animals did you bring her this time?" Roman asked snarkily. Hell yeah, he was judging Asher for trading life for life. He'd brought Blaire here thinking Odine could do a chant or feed her a magic potion, or hell, anything other than round two of raising her wolf.

"I brought her healthy ones, like I should've done the first time. It's probably your fault Blaire's wolf didn't take in the first place."

"You really are evil."

"Fuck you, Roman. I do what I have to do to protect the people I care about."

"And Gentry is one of those people? You've spent your whole life hating him."

"Yeah, well," Asher said softly as he stared off into the evening woods. "Not everything is as I thought. And it's not just Gentry either. Blaire's important."

Another wave of dark power pulsed from the house and made Roman want to yack in the snow.

Mila had looked scared earlier, and her cheeks were red like she'd been running. Maybe she had overexerted herself carrying Blaire through the woods, but Mila's mom—her ghost mom—had warned him that Mila was in trouble. She'd been standing right beside him outside of Jack's while Roman watched Rhett shove Mila into his truck. And then a vision of Mila walking through the Winter's Edge woods carrying Blaire had flashed across his mind, and her ghost mom had smiled sadly at him. That had never happened before, getting a vision of the future from a ghost. Rangeley wasn't good for avoiding his abilities. Being here was making them stronger. He needed to leave soon and get on with real, semi-normal life, but the thought of being separated from Mila made his wolf want to dig his claws in and stay.

"Roman," Asher said low. He jerked his chin toward the woods.

Roman followed his gaze to a gray-mottled wolf with white paws. She was lanky, petite, with a darker gray saddle and a black nose, and those beautiful champagne-colored eyes. Mila.

"What's a Bone-Ripper doing here?" Asher asked.

"She's fighting an order." Nope, he couldn't help the pride in his voice right now. Mila, submissive, bottom of one scary-ass pack, was here in wolf form, giving two silent middle fingers to Fuckface Rhett.

The door flew open behind them, and Odine's onyx-colored eyes trained immediately on the wolf. When she jammed a finger at Mila, she hunched down, flattening herself in the snow. Roman moved to stand between them, but Odine clipped out, "Sit and stay, Roman. I need her, too. Draw her closer, and we can fix this tonight. She's good. Good like Gentry. Blaire needs her." She spun to go back inside, but stopped, and turned suspicious eyes on the wolf, then cast her glance down to Roman. "You're making her sick."

Indeed, Mila was pacing back and forth, hackles flat, eyes empty, limping like her body hurt.

"I can take her bond from the pack," Odine said, arching a black eyebrow in question to Roman.

Mila ran into the woods and cowered there, just on the line of trees surrounding the clearing. Clearly, she wanted nothing to do with whatever Odine was offering.

Roman stood and blocked the witch's view of Mila. "Fuck with her, and I'll gut you, Psychodine. I'll be the one fixing her bonds if she wants that."

A curious and bone-chilling grin took Odine's face. "I believe you, Young Blood." She tapped her temple and winked. And then she turned and bustled into her cabin. Inside, she made her way to a table where Blaire and Gentry were laid beside each other like two corpses. Without anyone touching it, the door slammed closed.

When he turned around, Mila was right there, just a few feet away from him, shaking, belly low in the snow, smelling like pain, but she wasn't running anymore.

She was here, close to him, even though it made

her sick to disobey a direct order just so she could help Blaire.

Odine was right. She was good. Mila was so much more than he'd ever realized.

Roman wanted to pet her to see if her fur was as soft as it looked, or if was coarse like his own. Being closer to her would hurt her, though, so he climbed up to the top step beside Asher and leaned his back on the door. The draw of energy was so much worse here, but it was worth it if he could make Mila a fraction more comfortable.

And inside him, a big realization was happening.

As he stared at the wolf lying in the snow, he knew with certainty he would do anything to make her life easier. This was huge. Mila was the only person whose well-being he'd worried about over his own.

He was a survivor. Survivors were concerned with their own safety first, but not this time. He would take a bullet if it kept her safe from the reach of Rhett and the Bone-Rippers.

A storm is coming, the woods whispered. It was Odine's voice he heard, but a quick glance at Asher's passive face said it was all in Roman's head.

Lucky Mila. She'd earned the fealty of a psychopath.

The door opened so suddenly Roman fell backward. Since he felt like shit, he stayed there on the floor, arms spread like a starfish. Odine stood above him. "Is Blaire okay?" he asked.

"They both are."

"Good, I'm glad Mila wasn't here for that long." What had possessed him to say that out loud?

Odine rested her hands on her hips and angled her face as she stared down at him. "She's been lending me power for two hours Roman. Where was your head at?"

Roman sat straight up. "No, she just got here." Surely, he didn't just stare at her pretty wolf for two fucking hours.

Odine arched one eyebrow. "I'm tired, and you all need to eat and get some rest. Take your brother and the white wolf and go. She'll need to Change as soon as she feels strong enough."

"And Gentry?" Asher asked. He was hunched over weakly, his face hollow.

Odine stood to the side and gestured to Gentry, standing on his own two feet, lifting his mate off the table. He cradled her close to his chest and rocked her gently, murmuring something too low for Roman to make out. It was such an intimate moment that Roman wanted to look away, but couldn't. Gentry really loved her. The real kind of love Roman hadn't believed in until now. Until his own heart had started beating the moment Mila had told him, "You're going to get me hurt," in the Four Horsemen. It was the moment she flipped it on him. It was the moment she'd made the game real, because his protective instincts over her had reared up and urged him to burn the Bone-Rippers to ashes just because they scared her.

Mila stood weakly and limped off to the edge of the woods, and there she stayed, watching Roman like he was everything. Like she couldn't look away from him. What was happening to them? To him?

Roman ripped his gaze away from her. "Asher, you look like a corpse."

"I need meat," his oldest brother said in a hoarse voice as he stood, clutching the railing.

"That's what she said," Roman muttered. Geez he must've been drained. He didn't even feel like laughing at his own joke right now.

With Blaire folded in his arms, Gentry stepped around Roman, and wordlessly, he made his way to the Jeep. At the edge of the forest, Mila cried out. She'd Changed back, but apparently not on purpose. She had no clothes, and Roman could see the gooseflesh all over her skin from here. God, even bowed into herself she was beautiful. Flawless, pale skin, perfect curves, hair wild in the wind.

He was already running toward her. When Gentry tossed him the blanket from the floorboard in his jeep, Roman caught it without missing a step.

"I don't feel good," Mila said helplessly, but he was already wrapping her up in the blanket.

"It's okay. I'm gonna make it better."

"H-how?"

"Do you trust me?"

She wrapped her arms around her stomach and whispered, "I shouldn't."

****

Mila had hurt him with those words. She could tell, but it had come from an honest place. He had left her without saying goodbye and hurt her deeply. There wasn't an apology for abandoning her to this life without an explanation. There was no closure.

Roman could disappear in a moment, just like the ghosts she was pretty sure he could see.

Roman's frown was completely at odds with his normally smiling face as he walked her to the car, tossed Asher the keys, and pulled her onto his lap in the passenger's seat.

Her stomach hurt so bad, as if she'd drunk a gallon of gasoline and swallowed a burning match. Being in the car with all three Strikers made it even worse, but she drew comfort from Roman's strong arms around her. He pointed the heater vents right at her. He was colder than normal, but he was giving her all the warmth he could.

The trip to the Hunter Cove Inn was a silent one. Roman wouldn't look at her, but instead kept his gaze fixated on the white woods that blurred by outside. She wished she could say something witty like he always did. Something to make him laugh and ease the tension she'd caused with her admission.

Asher pulled to a stop in the frozen parking lot between the three cabins that made up Hunter Cove Inn. Gentry pulled Blaire from the back seat and carried her toward one of the smaller cabins. Asher made his way to the smallest, dilapidated cabin, and without a word, Roman slammed the jeep door behind him and carried Mila toward Noah Striker's old cabin—the one he used to refer to as ten-ten. Noah had always said there was magic in the number, but she'd always thought he was full of it. It was just an address. Good magic didn't exist.

"You live here now?"

Roman made a tick sound behind his teeth like he was frustrated. "Gentry, that dick muffin, made me take it after he moved into Blaire's cabin. He said it didn't feel right living in Dad's old cabin, so I got it by default. Lucky me."

Weakly, Mila smiled. "Noah always said the cabin was magic."

"Yeah well, magic just sucked like twenty years off all our lives, so I'm not a fan of otherworldly mojo, if you catch my drift. Mila, why shouldn't you trust me?" he asked suddenly.

So she *had* hurt him. "Because you're a leaver, Roman Striker. And thanks to Odine, I will always be a stayer."

Roman shook his head and gritted his teeth hard as he set her on her feet inside and closed the door behind him. It was warmer in here, but Mila still felt as cold as ice. She couldn't stop shivering.

Roman turned, and he was on her fast. His hand cupped her neck as he leaned down. His lips were urgent against hers, but she was so shocked she just stood there frozen. The sickness in her middle eased, but that made no sense. She was closer to Roman than ever. How many times had she dreamed of this moment when she was younger? How many times had she wished more than anything that Roman would kiss her like this? Mila softened her mouth and sucked on his bottom lip. A long, low growl rattled from Roman's throat. It should've terrified her, made her inner wolf cower, but right now, the fire that had been burning up her middle had transformed into a different kind of heat. Roman brushed his tongue against her lips, and she opened for him. The second his tongue touched hers, she let off a helpless whimper in desperation for more. Mila opened up the blanket and wrapped her arms around him.

His hand was strong and steady against the side of her neck, his thumb stroking her cheek as though she was precious. Nothing in the world had ever felt this right. Roman leaned down and lifted her up, wrapped her legs around his waist, then strode to the couch and settled on it. She thought he would grind up against her and start pushing for more. She wanted that, too, but he did something more profound. He slowed their kisses, slowed their pace, and ran his hands gently up and down her spine, trailing heat with his touch until she stopped shivering. He tasted so good. Smelled like cologne. She was so exhausted, she felt drunk with it, and her usual nerves were suffocated by the fatigue. She simply didn't have the energy to overthink this.

Roman shortened his kisses, made them softer, gave her tiny, sweet pecks until he eased away from her mouth and immediately pulled her against him. And they just sat like that, all wrapped up in the blanket together, their heartbeats racing, sharing warmth, as he massaged the back of her neck and pulled her hair gently as he petted her.

"Don't call me a leaver again," he murmured low. "I'm sorry I left before, but I'm not the same person I was back then. I was hurt, angry, and you scared me that night."

"What night?"

"At Jack's. I was already planning on leaving, and you were making me want to stay in that empty life.

Stuck in a small town, unable to join the pack, always being on the outside. I couldn't do it, Mila. And Asher was offering me a way out. He was kicked out, too, was leaving town, was starting from scratch, and it wasn't so scary because I wouldn't be alone. But if I stayed with you, figured out how important you were to me, to my wolf, all of it, you were going to realize what a fuck up I was, and I would be alone anyway. I had a chance to make a life, and I took it."

"You could've said goodbye."

"No, I couldn't. Mila, you don't understand. I couldn't. Saying goodbye wasn't an option. Another second with you, and I wouldn't have been able to leave. And what life could I give you? I was forced to be rogue, but you had a shot at the pack where you could be safe under my dad. You were loyal. Even at sixteen, you were so damn loyal, and I could see our future. You wouldn't pledge to the pack because you would worry for me. Leaving without that goodbye was the only gift I could give you."

"You didn't save me from anything, Roman. You were my friend. You and Asher and Gentry. After you all left, Rhett was watching me, always. Hunting me always."

"Why did Odine bind you to Rangeley?"

Mila's eyes burned, and she nuzzled her face against his throat to stop herself from crying. "I went to her to fix my wolf."

"What do you mean fix her?"

"I thought Odine could make me dominant. I hate being at the bottom of the pack, Roman. I *hate* it. Even the nice members don't realize how they treat me. It's like I'm this pathetic little girl who always needs to be taken care of. They talk to me like I'm stupid, or naïve. And Rhett had started the bullying already. I could see he was going to be alpha someday. Why wouldn't he be? He was brutal, and his wolf was Monster. And you Strikers had left this town unprotected. Your dad couldn't hold the pack forever. He was getting older, and Rhett was making me kiss him just to prove points. I asked the witch to fix me, and she bound me to Rangeley instead. It hurt, and it took three days. I couldn't get away from what she was doing, and now when I try to leave these mountains, I feel like I'm dying. I've tried every road out of here, every trail through the woods. I'm stuck. Stuck here, stuck in this life, stuck with Rhett always watching me, always hunting me. Roman," she whispered, easing back to cup his bearded jaw between her palms, "Rhett is going to make me alpha female."

Roman's eyes flashed gold. "Mila, you can't. You shouldn't. Never mind that Rhett will break you, the submissive wolf inside of you will buckle. There will be nothing left of you in six months."

"It's not up to me."

"Yes it is. You can say no."

"I did say no, Roman! I got out of his truck and ran from him. Ran into the woods. But how long do you think he will be patient with the hunt before he deems me expendable and ends me? He's done it before."

"What do you mean?"

She'd wanted to tell the Strikers the second she'd seen Gentry in town. She'd wanted to, but she'd been chicken, just like Roman always called her. He didn't know how accurate that nickname really was. "Your dad," she whispered.

Roman jerked his face out of her hands, but then pulled her palm to his lips and bit her gently as he stared at the wall. He shook his head slightly. With a soft kiss against her wrist, he growled out, "Rhett killed Dad in an alpha challenge."

"That's not true, and you know it, Roman. Deep down you always knew. Rhett pushed him out of his own pack, and then he murdered him. And…"

"And what?"

"Roman, we were all there." Mila closed her eyes against the memory of Noah being killed in the woods right outside of Winter's Edge. "Rhett made us watch so we wouldn't ever challenge him as alpha. Drake tried to stop it, but Rhett killed him, too. And that tactic worked. Any potential coup on Rhett's throne was shredded the second we watched him murder our alpha and then murder the Second. We're all stuck, Roman. Rhett is quicksand, and none of us can escape."

Roman rolled her off his lap and stood. He paced to the kitchen, scrubbing his hand in irritation down his bearded jaw. He jammed a finger at her. "You can."

Mila shook her head. Roman didn't understand how this town worked anymore. He didn't understand pack dynamics. "I can't."

"You want to break the bond to that asshole, Mila? You want to leave the Bone-Rippers? Leave

Rangeley? I can give you that."

Roman was speaking fast, not making any sense.

"I don't understand."

Roman flicked his gaze to her arm, hidden by the thick blanket, then back to her eyes before he murmured, "Yes, you do."

Realization slammed into her like a tidal wave. Slowly, Mila let the blanket fall away from her arm, which was now tingling with what he'd suggested. Mila didn't think much about the double layer of bitemark scars on the inside of her elbow. She'd gotten the first when she was eighteen and had pledged to Noah's pack, and the second, Rhett had given her when she pledged to the Bone-Rippers, moments after Noah had died.

"Pledge to me," Roman said in that sexy, deep timbre of his. The one that had always been so steady and confident. The one that said he was completely serious right now.

"Rhett will kill you."

"He'll try and fail."

She'd seen what he'd done to Noah and Drake. "Roman, he'll *kill* you. He has no honor. No feelings. No remorse. Rhett owns this town—"

"He doesn't own you! No one does. I can protect you, Mila. I have the means. I have the wolf to do it. My body can protect yours. I've trained it to."

"Roman," she murmured, already denying him. She cared about him so deeply she couldn't be the cause of his demise. Couldn't. It was her job to protect him. Job? Yes, that felt right. Roman had always been special, not only to her, but to her wolf. *Mate*. Roman was hers to protect. "We can't. If you take one of his wolves—"

"Think about it," he rushed out, striding for the door.

Running Roman was doing it again before she could get her rejection past her lips. "Roman!" she called, standing as he pulled open the door and let the frigid air in.

"The fridge is stocked. Eat. Odine says you need to eat."

"So do you! Where are you going?"

Roman gripped the handle to the door, but turned just enough to tell her, "I'm going to Winter's Edge. Just...think about it. Promise me." There was a desperation in his eyes she didn't understand, and when she was quiet too long, he said it again, louder.

"Mila, promise me."

His eyes were so gold it almost hurt to look at them, and his face looked fearsome, as if he were right on the verge of a Change.

"Okay," she whispered. "I promise."

The door clicked closed, and Roman was gone. Mila padded to the window to watch him stride for the dark trail in the woods that would lead him the back way to Winter's Edge.

The sickness was back. It nearly doubled her over, but it made no sense. Since he was getting farther away from her, she should be feeling better, not worse.

Or perhaps Odine wasn't the only one in this town with magic. Roman saw ghosts and understood darkness in a way she couldn't comprehend. He'd just offered her the world, and she'd never once questioned whether he could really make it happen.

Do you trust me?

She shouldn't, but with all of her heart, she did. Roman was different now. He wasn't the boy who had kept her at a distance. He wasn't the irresponsible jokester she'd thought him to be.

Risking his own survival, Roman Striker had just

offered the protection of his body as her ticket to freedom.

SEVEN

Roman finished the last bite of the fourth grilled cheese he'd made in the kitchen of Winter's Edge. Thankfully they were close enough to the Grand Opening that food was stocked. And booze. He took another long swig of his beer to wash down the rest of the sandwich and narrowed his eyes at the freezer door at the back of the kitchen. It was one of those massive, silver ones.

Once upon a time, Gentry had locked him and Mila in there. Seven Minutes in Heaven, and he'd waisted every damn second of it trying to escape. God, his childhood self was a pecker.

Mila had told him she'd hidden pictures in there. Was that why she'd chosen the freezer? Because of those seven minutes of Roman being a typical idiot? Maybe she remembered it differently. He hoped she did. He should've made out with her then just to see if she liked him as much as he'd liked her, but he'd been busy trying to distract himself with pretty humans at the time to keep from ruining sweet Mila.

Humans. A couple wild nights with a junior varsity cheerleader at the local high school was what had gotten him kicked out of the pack. Asher had been banging a human at the time, too. It was the big secret shame, and now Roman wanted to laugh at Asshole Dad because he'd been shagging Odine, who was not only a mother-frickin' black witch, but was definitely human. "Should've kicked yourself out of your own damn pack," Roman muttered, making his way to the freezer.

Furthermore, coming back to Rangeley had been one bullshit experience after another. His brothers went to brawling with him whenever they had a spare moment, the Bone-Rippers were a literal pain in his ass, Winter's Edge had taken a ridiculous amount of work to bring back to its former glory, Dad had apparently been freaking murdered, a black witch had stolen some of Roman's soul juice, and now

Mila was going to reject his one and only offer to be anyone's alpha. He'd seen it in her eyes. She was going to push him away, or run away, or maybe both. Maybe he was the stayer now, and she was the runner.

This town blew a bag of donkey dicks.

Everything had been so heavy lately. Not enough laughing, not enough smiling. It made him feel like he had man-PMS, which he was pretty sure was a thing. He'd researched it last week when Blaire went on her period. He'd been afraid her moodiness was catching. Yep, her hormones could fuck with him. The internet would never lie.

Roman flipped on the stereo system on his way to the freezer, and the Thong Song blared at full volume through the kitchen and bar. Ha. Perfect.

The freezer was big, and two of the walls were lined with shelves of boxes. It was all hamburger patties, cheese sticks, mushrooms, and pickles ready for the fryer. Giant boxes of frozen crinkle-cut french fries took up almost an entire wall. Where would Mila have put a few pictures?

He trailed his fingers over the frosted cardboard as he made his way to the back. He checked every label, but it was all just food. Maybe Gentry had cleaned it out and thrown it away accidently. Or not accidentally. Gentry wasn't a fan of Dad either apparently. Maybe he had done it on purpose.

Speaking of Dad, Noah-freaking-Striker was in here with him, staring, just like he always did. Only this time he wasn't staring at Roman. He was looking toward the corner at an old wicker picnic basket.

"Move," Roman muttered, waving his hand at the ghost as he walked through him. God, sometimes he imagined he smelled the old-man cologne Dad used to wear. He opened the lid to the basket and, bingo-bango, he had a winner.

On top, there was a black and white framed photo of Dad standing right in front of the Winter's Edge sign with a big grin on his face. He'd seen this one before.

Roman still felt a little shaky from whatever Odine had done to save Blaire and Gentry, but eating had helped, and before that, making out with Mila had super-helped. He could only imagine what kind of healing powers she would've given him if they'd had sex. Just the thought of her naked, straddling his lap, and how fucking hard it had been not to push for more gave him yet another boner. He should start counting them for the *Guinness Book of World Records*. He'd had like four hundred since he'd started crushing hard on Mila again. She should dress up like Viagra for Halloween.

Roman pulled an old crate from the wall and sat on it. Despite his breath fogging the air as he slid the picnic basket in front of him, he wasn't cold anymore. He pulled out the picture of Dad and wiped a healthy layer of frost from it before he lifted his beer to the ghost watching him and said, "Looking good Dad. You look happy in this one." Asshole.

The next one he hadn't seen before, and it made him draw up and set Dad's picture down gently on the floor beside the basket. It was one of Gentry leaning on the bar top in Winter's Edge talking to Tim. Gentry was maybe seventeen, smiling, the background darker because the walls were made of those stained logs, but there was a light right over Gentry's head, highlighting his dirty blond hair. He'd worn it longer back then.

The next picture was of Asher. He'd always been the tallest of the three of them, but this one made him look like a giant. He was in his baseball uniform, probably ten years old, high-fiving Dad as he stepped on home plate. He was lanky as hell, and the helmet looked too big, but he was grinning huge and looking right at the camera. He'd loved baseball until he couldn't control his wolf and Dad pulled him from the team.

"Roman?" Gentry called.

Roman cleared the emotion from his throat and yelled, "In here."

"I swear to God if you're jacking off in the freezer I'm going to kill you. That's a health code"—Gentry opened the door, and his eyes went right to the picture in Roman's hand—"violation."

"Apparently Dad had these hanging in the bar," Roman explained, lifting up the one of Gentry. Nope, he wasn't going to look at Ghost Dad right now because that geezer was probably looking at Gentry all lovingly like he was his favorite person on earth. Prodigal son and all.

"Wooow," Gentry drawled.

Asher appeared in the doorway and startled Roman. "God, Asher, creepy much? It's a bar, and you aren't hunting. Make a little noise, for fuck's sake."

Asher was smiling as though he'd scared him on

purpose. Clearly everyone was feeling recovered from the witchcraft.

"What are you doing here?" Roman asked.

"Blaire and Mila are apparently having a girls' night," Gentry explained, pulling up a crate. "Me and Asher were making Mila sick, but Blaire makes her feel better. Some alpha order technicality or something. She's supposed to stay away from Strikers, but Blaire isn't a Striker. Yet."

"The pawn shop is probably running a special on rings for the holidays," Roman offered, because he was romantic and all.

"Blaire and Mila are painting their toes together," Asher said with a disgusted look on his face as he leaned against the farthest wall with his arms crossed.

Roman snorted and tossed his oldest brother the baseball picture. "Look, Asherhole, Dad looks like he loves you in this picture."

"I remember this day," Asher said low, wiping his hand across the frame. His palm came back filthy, but there was the ghost of a smile on his lips. "I hit a homerun. Since you and Gentry made yourselves sick on beef jerky at the game, I couldn't go to the pizza party with the team after."

Roman high-fived Gentry and said, "Job well done."

Asher flipped them off with an empty smile on his face.

Gentry reached into the basket and pulled out the next picture. It was one of Roman in a yellow hard hat and a white T-shirt he was sweating through. He was up on a stack of logs. "This must've been the summer I worked on Nelda's crew. Geez, who took this picture?"

"Probably Nelda," Gentry answered. "She always went around with that old 35-millimeter camera, remember? And she would always bully us for group photos after every pack meeting. I never saw any of the pictures, but I remember her always clicking away on that thing."

Roman narrowed his eyes on the depths of the basket. "Well, looks like this is your chance to see some of Nelda's artwork." He pulled out a stack of pictures taken private-investigator style of Dad and Odine.

He flipped through them one at a time and flicked them onto the floor, where Asher squatted and picked up a few of them. "What the fuck?"

Some were of him and Odine having dinner at a place Roman didn't recognize. It wasn't in Rangeley. Some were of them sitting on Odine's front porch. She was smoking something, and he was laughing in most of them. One was of their backs to the camera, Dad's arm slung around Odine's shoulders as he kissed her temple. There were some branches in the way that said Nelda had been hiding in the woods. Some didn't have Dad in them at all, but were of symbols carved into the trees around Odine's cabin. And some were just of Odine...looking over her shoulder outside of the grocery store, fixing her make-up in her truck, laughing as she talked on the phone. The last one was of Dad and Odine sitting on the front porch of ten-ten, huddled under a blanket on the swing. They were both looking at each other, smiling the same way Gentry and Blaire smiled. The same way Mila made Roman smile.

Roman pulled out a stack of letters bound in twine. He opened the first addressed to Mila.

Run all you want. It only makes me want you more.
Rhett

The next one said,

Someday I'll make you scream for me. Your voice will sound so sexy, all hoarse and scared. Do you keep my letters, Mila? Do they make you think of me when you see them, when you touch them? Do they make you want to touch yourself? I like something physical of mine in your den. Keep them safe until I'm the one inside your den.

Rhett

And the next read,

I liked last night. Kissing you is fun when you try to bite me. Keep pushing, bottom bitch. I like when you fight.

Rhett

Bottom bitch. Bottom-of-the-pack bitch. Rage boiled in Roman's blood, and he barely controlled the urge to rip the vile notes to little microscopic pieces and take a piss over them.

Tomorrow night is the night. Shutting down Winter's Edge. We'll make it a party, trash the place. Be there at eight, or I'll take it as an act of treason on my pack.

Rhett

Whoa. Roman read that one out loud to his brothers, and then he read the next ones, too. "Bottom bitch, you weren't there when I came to see you today. Rhett. Or today. Where are you, Mila? I like this game. Rhett. I saw you with him. Saw it with my own eyes. You thought you could casually date, Mila? Wrong. His blood is on your hands. Don't push me again, or it'll be your blood next. Rhett."

"Jesus," Gentry murmured, looking sick. "I wonder who he killed?"

"Well, half the damn Striker Pack is missing," Asher murmured. "So I would venture a guess at all of those. Brian, Sam, Voigt, Robert, Matheson, Krueger, Drake—"

"Dad," Roman said quietly.

Asher nodded and wrung his hands between his knees from where he'd squatted down. "That hunter in the woods."

"Sick wolf plus serial killer human," Gentry gritted out. "No wonder the pack went to battle as soon as Rhett said to attack me and Blaire. They know good and well he'll kill them if they disobey."

"Why don't they leave then? Why don't they find another pack? A safer one?" Roman asked.

Asher shrugged and shook his head. "I don't know."

Roman read the last letter out loud as gooseflesh rippled across his skin. "Pack meeting at eleven in the woods behind Winter's Edge. No challenge, no wolves. That fucker dies dishonorably. I'll be the hand of justice tonight. Pack law will be upheld. Mixing with that human bitch ended his life years ago. Tonight he will be held accountable for all the disgusting things he's done. Noah has tainted this pack for long enough. It's my turn as king now. Be there behind me or die with him. Your choice. Pledges to the new Bone-Ripper Pack will happen right after Noah's last breath. Rhett."

Mila's handwriting was at the top. "This is the worst day of my life." And then she'd jotted down the date. It matched the day Dad died.

The basket was empty now. She'd put this here

for him to find, even before she'd known he would come back to Rangeley. She'd put this here out of desperation that if something happened to the pack and to her, there would be proof of what had gone so wrong in this messed up town.

Mila hadn't ever been Bottom Bitch. She'd been stronger than any of them.

Roman gripped the letters as his mind spun like a top. This was a huge risk, her leaving this here. If Rhett had caught her... *Geez, what did Mila do?*

Asher looked right at him as if he'd read his mind. "She just gave us the proof we need to go to war. Now who wants to take on this pack? Who wants alpha? Can't kill Rhett without taking his throne, so which one of us wears the crown?"

"Not I," Gentry said in a hard tone.

All Roman wanted was Mila. He'd be miserable as alpha over anyone but her. "Not I."

Asher swallowed hard and stared at the back wall, as if he could see Ghost Dad, too. "Not I."

EIGHT

"Are you sure you're okay to be by yourself right now?" Blaire asked. Her bright green eyes were worried.

Mila giggled and shook her head. "Blaire, you almost died, and you're worried about me right now?"

"I didn't almost die," Blaire scoffed. "I had everything under control." One handed, she turned the old worn steering wheel of a truck Gentry had bought last week. His other one had gone boom the night the Bone-Rippers had attacked him and Blaire.

"Blaire?"

"Yeah?" she asked, pulling into the parking lot of a fast food burger joint on the edge of town where Mila had parked her car earlier.

"About that night we hunted you… I didn't want to do that. I didn't have anything against you or Gentry. I just didn't have a choice."

"Why not?" Blaire asked softly.

"You are rogue—"

"No, I'm not. I'm with the Strikers."

"Who are all rogue. None of them have pledged to an alpha. They can go their separate ways tomorrow, and it wouldn't hurt them. But I'm bound to Rhett, and he can control me in a lot of ways. Noah Striker wasn't like that. He was a good alpha. Firm but kind. He was a protector, like his sons. My alpha is not. Anyway, I just wanted to say I'm sorry. I think about that night a lot. I'll go to my grave with regrets about it."

Blaire sighed and pulled into a parking spot next to Mila's Jetta, then turned to her. "I forgive you."

Mila closed her eyes for a moment and sighed. She hadn't realized how much she'd needed Blaire's forgiveness. She'd stood by for too long while Rhett had manipulated the town and the pack. "I'm really glad Odine was able to fix you."

Blaire snorted. "Yeah, I'm just peachy now. I'm

just waiting to, I don't know, turn into a four-headed turtle or something. That woman ain't right. I think she showed me actual Hell today."

Mila laughed and drew her knees up to her chest. "Did you know Roman calls her Psychodine? Like...to the witch's face, he says that."

"Yeah, he's not scared like he should be."

Mila blew on the window, fogging it with her breath, and drew a cartoon broomstick. "Odine confuses me. She does bad things, uses bad magic, but she seems to be devoted to helping the Strikers. Do you know she is keeping Rhett weak?"

There was a frown in her voice when Blaire asked, "What do you mean?"

Mila leveled her with a look. "Gentry nearly ripped his throat out when the pack came after you, but Rhett should've healed by now. Instead, his injuries still look awful, and he smells like Odine's magic. I don't even want to know the extent of her power. We didn't know she could do this kind of stuff until Noah died. She's been coming for the pack ever since."

"Has she come after you?" Blaire asked.

"Odine came after me years ago, when I was

twenty. She keeps me here. I can never leave."

"Why?"

Mila tried to remember the exact explanation Odine had given her. "She said because my destiny was here. She said Roman would need me someday."

"Whoa," Blaire murmured, rolling up the sleeve of her jacket to reveal her forearm covered in gooseflesh. "Mila, if Odine thinks you are Roman's destiny, maybe you are. She said the same thing about me and Gentry. Sure, she brought us together, but he's mine, Mila, and I'm his. Does Roman feel important to your wolf?"

Mila flopped her head back against the headrest. "He's always felt important."

There was a split second of hesitation before Blaire sang, "You're gonna have his baaaabies."

"Stop," Mila said with a giggle.

"I'm calling it. You'll have all boys, and they'll all come out little miniatures of Roman, cracking pervy jokes and fully bearded."

Mila wrapped her arms around her stomach as she laughed at the vision of it. "Little bearded babies would be so cuuute!"

"Do you know he eats his breakfast every

morning in his underwear? While wearing one of those fur lined hats with the ear flaps? It's ridiculous."

"What kind of underwear?" Mila asked, blinking innocently.

"Briefs. With his shoes untied. Every morning. I'm pretty sure he does it to annoy me. Asher said as much, too."

"He asked to be my alpha," Mila admitted suddenly.

Blaire coughed really hard. "What?"

"He offered to break my bond to Rhett and put it on him."

"Whoooah." Blaire gripped the steering wheel and stared out the front window at the burger joint. "Would that work?"

"I think so, but it would get him killed. Rhett's dangerous. That, and I'm bound to this place, and Roman is...well...Roman. Noah used to talk about all the places Roman lived. He doesn't stay put. He's a roamer. Saying yes means I ask him to stay bound to Rangeley, too, and surely you can see it. He doesn't like it here. I don't want to stick him in the cage with me just so I can keep him. I don't do well caged, but it would eat Roman alive."

"So what are you going to do?"

Mila pursed her lips and wiped away the broomstick drawing. "I'm going to get in my car, drive home, sleep like the dead, work my shift tomorrow, and think this all through. Maybe I'll have more clarity away from Roman."

"Ha! I used to think that would happen for me, too, but mostly I just thought of Gentry the entire time I was away from him. Good luck with that."

Mila shoved the door open, got out, closed it, and turned to leave, but Blaire rolled down the window. "Hey Mila? I just wanted to say thank you."

"For what?" She was part of the reason Blaire had been sick in the first place.

"For helping me in the woods when I didn't feel good, and for helping Odine save me. She said you made the difference. Soooo…I don't really know much about how this werewolf stuff works, but I don't have a lot of friends in town, and I have exactly zero girlfriends, so if you ever want to…I don't know…hang out and Change into wolves together and run around the woods or hunt a bunny or something, I would be totally fine with that."

Mila laughed and leaned onto the window. "Blaire, are you asking me on a friend date?"

"Yeah." Blaire grinned. "Like a werewolf friend date."

Mila scanned the parking lot to make sure they weren't being watched by any of the Bone-Rippers and then pulled out her cell phone and saved the number Blaire recited for her. "I'll call you," Mila promised as she walked away.

"Or a turkey," Blaire called as Mila got into her car. "I like those, too."

As Mila turned on her Jetta to warm it up and watched Blaire drive away, a strange feeling drifted through her. Was this...was it hope? It had been a while since she'd felt that emotion, but yes, it seemed right. Blaire wasn't as submissive as Mila, but she wasn't overwhelmingly dominant. She was happy and funny, and maybe if Mila was really careful not to get caught, she could hang out with the White Wolf of Winter's Edge. And maybe that would be more of an excuse to accidentally see Roman, too.

She had to say no to Roman's offer to be her alpha, but she couldn't help but imagine how it could be. He would be good to her. Protective. Maybe over time, he would even grow to care for her like she cared for him.

Sure, Rhett threw a wrench in everything, but still, it was fun to imagine a better life with Roman. One where Rhett didn't exist.

She coasted through town in a daze as her mind spun around all that had happened today, but as she passed her old house on Marina Road, someone tall, muscled, sexy, and bearded caught her attention. Roman was out in the front yard of Regina Delphine's house, building something giant in the snow.

"What in the hell?" she murmured, pulling over to the curb. She poked the automatic window button and waited for it to roll all the way down before she asked, "What are you doing?"

Roman packed on one more handful of snow, then turned with a grin. "Come here and look at the present I made for you."

There were two giant snow balls on either side of a tall cylinder shape. Oh, dear God, Roman had built a giant dick, complete with circumcision and pee-pee hole. Mila died laughing, and Roman's grin grew bigger as he rested his hands on his hips and stared at her with those bright blue dancing eyes of his.

Still cracking up, Mila got out and jogged over the yard to him.

"Okay, okay, wait," Roman said between laughs. "There is a story behind this."

"Illuminate me, please," she gasped out, clicking pictures with her phone. She made sure to include Roman because he was wearing her favorite smile along with a plain white T-shirt, jeans that were caked in snow, and heavy boots. He looked hot as hell right here in the middle of a Maine winter.

"So I went to Blaire because I had questions."

"What kind of questions?" she asked, playing along.

"I said, 'You have tits and a vagina...'"

"God, here we go…and what did she say?"

"She said, 'Yeeeees.' Just like that, she drew out the word, and her face was all scrunched up like a squirrel and suspicious looking. And then I said, 'So you understand girl stuff.' And she mushed up her face even more and said, 'I guess.' So then I said, 'How do I get a girl to want to...' And since she's smart and uses all these big words, I figured she'd get what I was saying."

"I don't even get what you're saying."

"So then I said, 'How do I get a girl to suck my dick for life.'"

"Roman! Wait." Realization slammed into her. "Sucking your dick for life? Were you talking about me?" That was the sweetest thing he'd ever said.

"Focus, Chicken. So then Blaire said, 'Aaaaw,' and looked ridiculous and mushy, made me want to barf, but then she told me I should do a grand gesture for you." Roman held out his hand like Vanna White to the giant dick. "And I can't think of anything grander than an eight-foot snow penis in your front yard."

The light flipped on in the house, and Mila couldn't help her laughter if she tried. Roman looked proud as a rooster.

"It's the greatest gift anyone has ever made for me," she forced out past her giggling, "but this isn't my yard anymore."

The smile fell from Roman's face so fast she peeled into laughter all over again.

"I moved out of this house when my dad moved to Michigan. Mrs. Delphine lives here now."

"Ooooooh," Roman said, biting back a smile. "That's kind of funny, but it's also kind of bad. She never liked me."

"You toilet papered her house every Saturday for three months straight, Roman. She hated you." Mila rested her hands on his chest right over those perfectly puckered nipples. She could feel the cold metal of his piercings through the fabric. She was turned on, but even more than that, she was feeling mushy, just like he'd described Blaire. This was a really sweet gesture in a Roman-esque way. He was out here in the middle of the night, in the freezing cold, building her a snow-pecker.

Hope bloomed a little bigger in her chest.

Mila lifted up on her toes and kissed his lips as she slid her arms slowly up his chest and around his neck. Geez, how was he this warm? Sure, she ran warm, too, thanks to the wolf, but Roman ran hot as fire. He angled his head and pushed his tongue past her lips as he gripped her waist. His thumb brushed her bare skin under the hem of her shirt, and oooh, her body was melting from the center outward right now.

"What in tarnation is that?" Mrs. Delphine yelled from her front porch.

Mila and Roman froze, lips locked, unmoving like they both thought Mrs. Delphine was some movement-seeking raptor who would catch onto them if they even breathed.

"Roman Striker? Is that you?" She wrenched her voice up so high it hurt Mila's ears so that she had to hunch her shoulders.

Roman disengaged with a soft smack sound. He was grinning. "We should go."

"Yep."

"I'm calling the police!" Mrs. Delphine hollered as Roman guided Mila back to the car at a speed-walk.

Mila was trying not to laugh, she really was, but when he closed Mila's door the second she was safely inside, he remorselessly called, "You have a good night, Mrs. Delphine!" as he strode toward his silver Wrangler parked across the street.

Mila giggled the entire way to her house with Roman's headlights glaring into her car as he followed her. Gosh, today had been the best day. And it wasn't even over yet! Sure, it had been a complete roller coaster—breakfast with Roman, Rhett's terrifying alpha female proposal, Blaire getting sick, the witch's house, the recovery, and the fun little girls' night with Blaire. And now the snow-penis? She couldn't even remember the last time she felt happy like this. Or safe, which was a really big deal. But right now, with Roman so close, she wasn't even worried about the pack. She was just excited to see him again, touch him again, and kiss him again. She hadn't laughed this much in...well...since she'd hung out with Roman when they were kids.

When she pulled into the driveway of her little rental house, painted daffodil yellow with white trim, she checked the pictures on her phone to make sure she got good ones of Roman's present. She couldn't take her eyes from Roman, smiling so big, looking at her as though he'd missed her. As though she was beautiful. He looked so happy. Did she make him feel like he made her feel? Light with moments of utter freedom? He had the best smile. The best in the world. Big grin, laugh lines at the corners of his bright blue eyes, straight white teeth, and that sexy beard. She hadn't ever really liked facial hair until Roman.

With a happy little squeak, she pushed open her door, and he was there, her knight in shining nipple bars. She should feel sick right now with Rhett's orders, but she didn't. Maybe Roman had good magic.

"Hi," she said, feeling a little less brave, and a little shyer, as she stood looking at him.

"Hey, Chicken, don't freeze up on me now. You were doing good back there."

Her cheeks flushed at the compliment as he gripped her waist and eased her back against the car. "I liked how *you* kissed *me*. You didn't hesitate. I know it's not in your nature to do what you want with a dominant, but that's how I can tell you like me."

"I do like you." Mila wished her voice didn't shake when she said it, but that couldn't be helped. He was making her whole body shake. Not in fear, but in anticipation.

Roman angled his face and frowned slightly, then pulled her closer to him gently and rested his cheek onto hers. He inhaled deeply and just stood there, holding her. Whatever he was doing worked because she settled. No…her wolf settled.

And a sudden fear seized her. She was falling so hard, so fast, but he was a temporary fixture here. This was going to hurt when he left. It was going to cut much deeper than she was prepared for. "I think I like you too much," she whispered.

"You don't. You can't. There's no such thing as too much."

"But I get tempted to say yes."

Roman rubbed his beard against her cheek and plucked at her earlobe with his lips. "Yes to me breaking your bond?"

"Mmm hmm," she murmured, closing her eyes against how good his lips felt on her ear. That had always been a sensitive spot for her, and somehow Clever Roman had found it right away.

When he brushed his tongue softly against her lobe, Mila let off a helpless sound and melted against his chest completely.

"When you're ready, tell me, and I'll fix it, Mila. I'll fix what's happening, keep you safe. I'll protect you from Rhett, from the pack, from Odine, from everything."

What a beautiful promise, whispered right there in her ear, ringing with honest notes that said Roman truly believed he could be her protector. And she trusted him. He was strong. She'd seen him fighting the pack, trying to keep Blaire safe with his brothers. He'd been the ripper. She hadn't been able to take her attention from his deadly grace.

Roman eased away and slid his big, strong hand around hers, then led her up to the door. "Are you as big a slob as you were when you were a kid?" he asked.

Mila giggled and shoved his shoulder gently. "No. I keep a clean den."

"Not me. I like chaos."

"Deal-breaker," she teased. "We wouldn't ever work, Roman. I can't live in clutter."

"Oh, that's the deal breaker? Chicken, you'll find out a hundred worse things about me that'll make you want to run. My tidiness won't even be a blip on your radar."

"Like what?" she asked as she shoved the key in the door and opened it.

"Like I talk in my sleep. Or so I'm told. I don't wake myself up. I tell stories, but with words that don't make sense."

"Casting spells?" she joked, but when she looked over her shoulder, Roman was frowning.

"Something like that." He stepped inside and flipped on the light switch beside the door.

Mila inhaled deeply, searching for her bravery, and pushed his chest until his back was up against the wall. "Tell me something else. Something real."

Roman looked truly disturbed when he

whispered the next admission. "Today when I knew you were in trouble? Your mom was the one who told me."

Mila froze. Once upon a time, in the woods when they were kids, he had talked about her mother. She had thought he'd meant to hurt her, but now she knew he hadn't. Some instinct told her Roman had many demons, and one of them was that he could see beyond the veil. What torture. Mila hugged his waist and rested her cheek against his drumming heartbeat. "I know you see them, Roman. I wish you didn't."

"They go away when you touch me," he said in a gravelly voice.

Mila looked up at him, resting her chin against his sternum. She couldn't help her smile. "Really?"

Roman searched her face as he brushed her bangs to the side. "Odine isn't the only one with magic, Mila. You have the good kind inside of you. The kind that makes the darkness inside of me feel smaller."

Mila's stomach was filled with the fluttering sensation of butterflies. Roman was spilling something important. No jokes, no running. He was here with her, admitting deep, dark secrets.

"What else?" She wanted to hang onto his every word.

"I was born human."

Mila blinked hard and shook her head. That, she would've never expected in a hundred years. "What? How?"

"I just found out recently. My mom was human, and my brothers and I were all born human. Odine put wolves in us. It's what my dad wanted. He didn't want human sons. It's why our animals are all fucked up. There are…side effects to her magic."

"Is that why you see ghosts?"

Roman dipped his chin once.

Mila pressed her palm against his heart. It was beating way too fast. "Are you afraid that will matter to me?"

Another dip of his chin.

"Well, it doesn't. You feel all wolf to me. Is that all?"

A slow, wicked smile took his lips. "That, and I tell a hundred dick jokes a day."

She huffed a soft laugh. "I find dick jokes funny."

"God, you're perfect," he growled.

Mila giggled as he plucked at her neck with his lips and backed her toward the couch.

"You always were," he said right before he kissed her.

Easing back, she asked, "Then why didn't you show any interest?" She'd always wondered. He'd been hot and cold when they were growing up, toying with her at times.

"Because you were good, Mila. It wasn't that I didn't find you pretty. You're gorgeous. It wasn't that I didn't find you funny or I didn't think about you when you weren't around. I could feel something was wrong. With me. And I didn't want the bad parts of me stealing the good parts of you."

"And now?" she asked breathlessly as he bit her throat gently.

"Now, I want you to be the big bad wolf... Just." *Kiss.* "Like." *Kiss.* "Me."

A shiver trembled up her spine, and a soft growl rattled her throat. Roman eased back and cupped her neck, gently pressed his thumb over her throat to feel her growl. He smirked down at her as if she'd done something he was proud of. "That's my girl."

Mila's breath was coming faster now, but she

could do this. Roman was telling her he liked her wild, telling her he liked when she did what she wanted to him. So she slid her hands under the hem of his T-shirt and ran her palms up the defined ridges of his abs to his chest, then up to his shoulders and back down to those nipple bars.

She flashed him a look just to make sure he was still in this as she lifted up his shirt. He was a lot taller than her, so he gave a crooked smile and pulled it off the rest of the way. And then he laid on the couch, on his back, dragging her with him. It was a really submissive position for a dominant man like him, so it took a second for Mila to wrap her head around this. Was straddling his lap okay? Roman was looking up at her with that devilish grin that said he was waiting to see what she did with this, and it made her a little braver.

Scrunching up her face, she closed her eyes and pulled her jacket off as quickly as she could. Her sweater came next, and then she crossed her arms over her bra as she eased one eye open. It was really bright in here right now.

Roman pulled her arms gently away from her chest and arched his eyebrows. "No need to be shy with me, Chicken. I love everything about you. It's just you and me, and we're having fun. No one's judging." He reached forward and unsnapped the front clasp on her bra, then pushed it back off her shoulders.

As much as she wanted to close her eyes again and hide, Mila forced herself to watch his face. His slow, hungry smile made the effort worth it. Roman lifted up to a sitting position and kissed her, pushed his tongue past her lips and stroked it against hers. His hand was at the back of her neck, keeping her close, but she didn't feel trapped. Instead, she felt...safe.

She let off a relieved sigh at the warmth of his skin touching her tingling breasts. God, this was everything, coveted by the man who'd always felt so big, wrapped in his arms, kissed and taken care of... protected. She let any feelings of insecurity go. Roman liked this, liked her. His erection was hard as a stone between them, and she rolled her hips against it. That was all the hint Roman needed. He immediately took them back down to the couch, her laying on top of him, and lifted her up enough to shimmy out of his jeans. Much more clumsily, and with a few giggles on her part and chuckles on his, Mila struggled out of her shoes and pants until she was wearing only a pair of pink lace panties.

"There," she said, straddling him breathlessly, her cheeks on fire.

"Yeah, I'd say we're there," Roman murmured, staring between her thighs as he gripped her waist so hard his fingers dug into her skin. Felt good. "You gonna ride me now or what, Chicken?" he murmured in a deep, gravelly voice.

Her middle turned molten at his naughty words, and she rocked her hips to reward him. "Maybe. Or maybe I'll go all submissive and make you do the work."

"Oh, no," Roman said, his grip on her hardening as he pulled her in a stroke up his erection. "Big bad wolf with me, remember?" His eyes went serious. "Make me forget the ghosts for a little while."

He thought she was some kind of magic, but she wasn't. She was just Mila, plain, simple, boring, bottom-of-the-pack Mila. But the way Roman was looking at her made her feel like so much more. She leaned forward and clamped her teeth on his chest, right over his heart. Roman hissed and arched against the couch, but was holding the back of her head as though he enjoyed the rough play. So she bit him harder, bit him until she could taste the faintest hint of iron, and then she released him and licked the bite mark slowly. Roman was rocking his hips against her now as if he couldn't help himself, and his eyes flashed bright gold.

Hello wolf. My wolf. My mate.

A ripping sound filled the air, and then her panties were gone, floating from Roman's fingertips as he tossed the shred of lacey fabric to the floor. Sexy man, and now there were no barriers separating their skin. She was sitting right over his thick erection and, good God, it felt so perfect as he rolled through her wet folds.

"Roman," she pleaded.

"You don't have to beg, Mila. You're in control," he answered. "You can do whatever you want."

Oh. Right. Mila lifted up slightly and guided him to her entrance, then slid down him slowly, fingers clawing his chest as she panted shallowly. He was big…almost too big…but she'd been ready for him, relaxed.

Roman's hand went to her ass now and she set the pace slow to let her body adjust to his size. With his other, he gripped the back of her neck and pulled her to him, kissed her until she felt drunk. They were moving together now in this perfect rhythm that was so easy, so natural, like their bodies already knew each other, knew what the other needed.

Mila was already close, the pressure building too fast in this position. "Roman," she squeaked out helplessly.

"Come for me," he growled against her lips, then bit her bottom one as he squeezed her ass and rammed her down harder onto his dick.

Well, that did it. There was no putting off the orgasm that exploded through her. Her entire body was taken with it as she slid up and down him and sank her teeth into the bite mark she'd made earlier. Felt right.

Roman snarled and flipped her over on her back so fast her stomach dipped. And then he reared back and slammed into her, his elbows resting on either side of her cheeks, his hands pushing her bangs back, his wild gold eyes locked on hers, trapping her in his gaze. His teeth were gritted, too sharp, face feral, sexy

Roman. He was pushing into her fast, and her orgasm was somehow getting stronger as her body became more sensitive to his. She cried out, and when she clawed his back, Roman bucked into her and ground out her name, freezing as his dick pulsed warmth inside of her. He reared back and pushed in again, and more warmth, more and more.

He didn't bite her like she had him, but Mila knew why. He wanted her to ask him. He wanted her to give consent for the bite that would take Rhett's bond away. Maybe he didn't want to do it during sex and wanted a formal ceremony instead, she didn't know, but she wasn't hurt by his lack of teeth.

He was taking care of her now. Kissing her, running his fingers over her skin, exploring her body as he moved slowly within her, drawing out both of their releases and making sure she felt adored.

Roman had done something incredible for her tonight. He'd put her in a dominant position and asked her to own it. And she had. She was proud of herself for the first time in a long time. He'd done that for her. Did he even realize how important it was that she felt in control for once?

She wasn't a phoenix yet, but for the first time in

a long time, she felt like, someday, maybe she could be.

NINE

Mila pulled out the old shoe box in the top corner of her closet. It was a box she had decorated like a robot when she was in grade school. There was a hole cut out on the top for the mouth, and during a Valentine's Day party, the other kids in the class had put their cards for her in it.

"Do you remember these?" she asked Roman.

He was sitting on the bed, the sheets around his hips as he rested his elbows on his knees. "Third grade, Mrs. Vandaveer's class, you won all the awards for you robot. I was so jealous because the awards were those bags of trail mix, and I wanted the M&Ms out of them so bad."

"You were super mean to me and said my robot

was ugly. I kicked you." She laid on the bed on her stomach, and Roman grabbed her bare ass and squeezed.

"Can I put on clothes yet? It's kind of cold."

"Bullshit, you're a werewolf. No. I like you like this. We said we were going to have an all-night naked party, and you're following through, Chicken. I'm keeping you honest."

She giggled and shook her head. He liked playing, and surprisingly, so did she. Roman made things fun again. "Anyway, I kicked you, and I was really proud, but you told on me, and Mrs. Vandaveer sent me to the principal's office. I was so upset. I'd never been before. And then I remember sitting in the chair outside of the principal's office just...shaking. The door opened, and in you came. You sat right beside me and held my hand. You said you hit Martin Kramer in the eye and got sent in."

"I didn't."

"What?"

Roman laid on his side, resting his elbow on the mattress, his cheek on his palm. "I didn't hit Martin."

"Then why did you get sent to the principal's office?"

"I didn't do anything bad. I asked to go to the bathroom, and then I came to sit with you because I knew you would be scared. I felt bad because I deserved the kick, and you were going to get in trouble for it."

Mila swallowed a few times, stalling as she ducked her gaze to the robot box. Well, that changed things. "What else did you do that I didn't know about?"

A smile crept across Roman's face. "Remember that dickface, John Cog, that you dated freshmen year in high school?"

"Pervy John?"

"Yeah, he broke up with you because I threatened to drag his ass up the water tower and pitch him off. I would've done it, too. Remember that football game where I caught you two arguing out near the back fence? He was pushing you too much, putting too much pressure on you, and you had your eyes on the ground, talking too quiet. He was going to get his way, and I wanted to pluck his intestines through his belly button. I didn't, though. I kept my crap together long enough to tell you I needed to talk to you about something important, alone, remember?"

"Yeah, and when John left, all pissed and cussing up a storm, you took me to the concession stand and bought me nachos with tons of extra jalapeños, like you knew exactly how I liked them without even asking. And then I asked what you wanted to talk about, but your eyes were gold, and you wouldn't answer."

"Because I was so angry with that prick, wanted to kill him, hated the way he'd been treating you at school. And I was scaring you, I could tell, because you couldn't make yourself sit close to me. And everyone around us was cheering for a touchdown, but I was watching you, thinking how pretty you were, and you gave me this little sideways look, a little smile, and you shoved the container of nachos across the metal seat toward me like it was your little thank you for getting you away from John. It was the first time I had shared food with anyone. And I remember there was this moment where I wished you were mine because I would never make you feel like John did. Like you didn't have a say. I wanted to scoot over and put my arm around you, tell you how much I liked you, but your mom appeared right between us. She was staring at me with this hollow look, and she shook her head and said, 'Not yet.' So I stayed put, not because your mom told me to, but because I could *see* your mom. John wasn't good for you, but neither was I. On Monday at school, I followed him into the bathroom and scared him into ending it with you because I knew you wouldn't do it. Not with a guy like that. He would bully you into taking him back just because you were soft-hearted. I wanted you to move on. I wished you could move on with me, but I wanted you happy, so I was good with you just finding someone nicer. Maybe one of the other boys in the pack. Maybe Gentry. I saw you watching him sometimes. John was going to grow up a brawler, I could feel it. My wolf hated him. He felt off. Sick. He felt like Rhett does now. I was glad when his parents moved him out of state the next year. I didn't want him to pledge to my dad's pack with you."

Mila scooted closer and rested her toes against his. The sheets separated them, but Roman smiled and leaned forward, kissed her gently. And then he plucked the lid off the robot box that sat on the bed between them. "What did you bring me, Chicken," he murmured as he stared at the top picture.

"Memories."

He pulled out the top photo and chuckled. It was a picture of her and the three Striker brothers standing in front of a bonfire. She was a year younger than Roman, and a lot shorter. He had his arm around her, his giant palm resting on her head, and was grinning. His other arm was around Asher, who was lanky and even taller. Gentry was standing by himself a few feet off, arms crossed, frowning at something off in the woods. Asher almost wore a smile, but it was her and Roman's face she loved in this one. They looked so happy, mid-laugh as though he'd just told a joke. He was looking at her, but Mila was looking at the camera, her eyes dancing.

"I remember this night," he said low. "I wish I could remember what I said to make you laugh like this."

"I'm sure it was gross."

"Oh, a hundred percent chance it was. It was a pack meeting, and we all cooked hotdogs on that fire. You cooked me one."

"You said it was too burnt."

"It was just right. I just liked to give you shit and watch your cheeks go pink. And then you made Gentry one, and I wanted to fight him. Oooh, I was mad. Dad had been on a tear, making sure everyone knew he was the favored son, the future alpha, and Asher was in my ear reminding me all the goddamn time how bad it sucked to be us. To be the forgotten sons. And here was Gentry, getting something from you that I had thought was just for me."

"I didn't mean to do that. I just felt bad for not offering him one, too. I asked Asher, too, but he said he didn't like people doing stuff for him. You and Gentry always let me take care of you a little, though. I liked doing that. It made me feel important, like you two wouldn't let Asher get rid of me because I had value. Because I could do little things to make you smile. And anyway, you were dating that Christie human at the time. I'd seen you sneaking off with her. I hoped you were just friends, but it still hurt that you would pick a human over me. I was going to be in your pack, and we got along well. I l—" Mila cleared her throat and tried again. "I liked you. A lot. And you were choosing a human. You were choosing the human that would get you kicked out of the Striker Pack. And I freaking told you, Roman. You were being reckless, being too obvious with her. When you got caught, it was an awful day."

"You were one of the only ones who knew the real reason behind me and Asher getting banished from the pack,' Roman said softly as he brushed her bangs to the side with the tip of his finger. "Dad was so ashamed. I was dating Christie—"

"More than dating. You got caught having sex with her. With a human. That's the biggest rule, and you broke it. You risked everything for her. And when Asher's girlfriend outed him to Tim a few days after you were caught, it felt like the world had flipped on its axis. I knew your dad wouldn't be able to get out of punishing you both severely. That pack meeting… Roman, I saw you break, and I broke right along with you."

Pain rippled across his face, and for once, it was Roman who ducked his gaze. "It was a mistake. It was me spiraling. I was seeing more and more ghosts. They were seeking me out, and I was never alone. They would stand in my bedroom just watching me at night, like they were waiting for me to go to sleep, and I couldn't tell anyone about it. Couldn't admit how crazy I was. Christie was rebellion from the stuff I was going through, but also from Dad. And the longer I dated Christie, the more I thought I was invincible. Or maybe I wanted to get caught, I don't know. Sometimes that feels right because, at the time, I wanted my dad to see me. He never looked at me or Asher. Never saw us. I was like one of the ghosts that followed me around...invisible. Nothing I did got his attention. Asher didn't try, but I thought if I was funny enough, and outgoing enough, Dad would realize I was as good as Gentry. And when that didn't work, I found another way."

"Christie?"

Roman nodded. "Pretty stupid, huh? I threw away my whole life on a girl I didn't even care about, and who didn't care about me."

"Or maybe this was how it was supposed to be," Mila said, pushing old movie stubs and concert tickets aside for the next picture. It was one she'd taken out at the bluffs. They'd gone hiking for hours and ended up on top of a ridge, overlooking miles of rolling hills. All three Strikers were sitting near the edge, their backs to the camera, the sunset painting the sky in front of them. Roman and Asher were sitting beside each other, but Gentry was yards away, all on his own. They all sat with their knees drawn up, arms resting on them, but while Roman and Asher looked relaxed as they talked, leaning their heads toward each other, Gentry's back was tense, and he looked like he had no friends in the world.

"You said I used to watch Gentry. It wasn't because I cared for him like I did you, Roman. It was because he was alone. Your dad did him no favors by favoring him. He cut him off from the two of you, and I could see him longing to be a part of the relationship you and Asher shared. He had no shot in hell at that the way things were. But since you've come back to Rangeley, I see a difference. One that makes my heart happy, not only for Gentry, but for you. You three went to war with the Bone-Rippers. Together. You three came into the Four Horsemen and declared your place as the Wolves of Winter's Edge. Together. And then you and Asher took Gentry to Odine's and sat outside for him, allowing that witch to take from you to give to him. And you fought for his and Blaire's life. Together. Sometimes things need to break all the way before they can be put back together again. Maybe your relationship with your brothers isn't the same as if you had all been whole in the first place." Mila shrugged. "Or maybe fighting for those relationships will make them even better."

TEN

Head down, focus, don't meet their eyes.

Mila tucked in the long-sleeved, black Four Horsemen work T-shirt into her jeans as she passed Tim, Nelda, and Frank talking quietly at one of the tables. She purposefully kept her face angled away from the pool table in the back where Rhett was breaking on a new game. He hit the balls so hard one jumped off the table, and Mila hunched at the explosive sound.

"Mila," Rhett called in a stone-hard tone. "Come play a game with me."

"Um, no thanks," she murmured, making a beeline for the kitchen. "I have to get on the clock."

"Now," he gritted out.

She stared at her boss, Tim, silently pleading with him to make her get to work. He looked regretful about it, but he twitched his head toward Rhett and murmured, "Go on, girl. Your alpha's calling you."

Great. As she meandered around the maze of tables toward Rhett, Mila couldn't help but think about how the Strikers would've reacted to her quiet plea for help. They weren't a pack, just four separate rogues including Blaire, but any one of them would've helped her out. They would've told Rhett to fuck off, maybe broken a pool stick against his face if he pushed too hard.

It had been like that under Noah when they were still the Striker Pack. Everyone had each other's backs, but the Bone-Rippers were such a broken pack. Rhett's darkness had trickled through the ranks and slowly poisoned every last one of them. They were all in survival mode thanks to Rhett's murderous tendencies, and now it was every wolf for himself.

All of this was easy to see with just a few days of spending time with the Strikers. They felt like potentially healthy relationships, and she'd started longing for normal. Or if not normal, whatever the

Strikers could offer her. Laughter, loyalty, protection, fun, a sense of belonging. And now every time Rhett pushed his dominant alpha shit onto her, it made her angry. Not sad or helpless anymore, but instead it made her blood boil. All she wanted to do was put her head down, work her shift tonight, and earn some tips so she could pay the rent she was already two weeks late on, thanks to him chasing out all the human clientele from this place.

Everything Rhett touched turned to ash.

If she gave him half a chance, he would turn her to ash, too.

She plucked a pool stick carefully from the wall and put chalk on the end, keeping her eyes averted, but she could feel his gaze on her. It lifted the fine hairs all over her body.

"You weren't home last night."

"I had plans."

"With me! I was going to take you out, remember? Mind the rules, court you before we made the announcement at the pack meeting, but low and behold, I show up to your place, and you weren't there. And don't you think for a goddamned second that I forgot you ran from me. I should've run you over with my fucking truck for disobeying me. Tell me you didn't see *him*."

Pleading the fifth, Mila lined up her shot and missed like a champ, her hands were shaking so badly.

"You did, didn't you?" Rhett's face was terrifying. His dark hair made his wolf-bright blue eyes look even lighter, and his face had gone red with fury as he slammed the pool stick against the edge of the table and locked his arms on the felt surface. "Fucking whore Bottom Bitch."

"I'm not."

"What?" he asked, his dark eyebrows arched high.

"I'm not those things," she forced out past her tightening throat.

Rhett leapt over the pool table and came crashing down on her, hands hard on her shoulders as he pushed her backward. When she slammed into the wall, he was right there, his lips an inch from hers, his smile feral. "Good, Mila. Stick up for yourself and see what it does for my desire."

Mila jerked her face away from his and tried to shove him off her, clawing at him as she did.

"Yeah, keep scratching at me and see how much

restraint I keep. Bottom. Bitch."

Mila's wolf raged inside of her. It was overwhelming and made her dizzy, but she would rather Rhett kill her and dump her body in the woods than be his bitch. She reared back and slapped him. "Let go of me," she gritted out, looking him dead in the eyes. Sure, her voice came out terrified and shaking, but she'd gotten the words out without choking on them.

Rhett's smile turned evil, and he squeezed her neck as he leaned forward and whispered in her ear, "It's going to be so fun to break you, Mila."

She thrashed out of his grip and shoved off him. Tossing him a last fiery glance, she made her way past the three pack members still sitting at the table in the center of the bar. "Fuck you all for not stopping that." She wanted to spit on the floor, but she would be the one cleaning it up, so stopped herself.

Tim, Nelda, and Frank stared at her like she'd grown an extra head, but fuck it all, she was done being treated like crap. She was done with how this pack worked, done with the bullying, done with the fear. An irate corner of her mind thought it would've been so much better for the pack if Gentry had actually succeeded in killing Rhett. If Asher hadn't jumped in and stopped him, if Rhett had bled out on the side of that snowy road. Maybe Gentry didn't want to be alpha, but anyone would be better than Rhett.

When she reached her station to clock in, the front door flew open so hard it slammed against the wall. Roman strode in looking like a hellion, eyes blinding gold, shoulders tensed and pressing against his sweater. His hair was mussed, and he held up a stack of different colored papers. "What the fuck are these, *alpha*?"

Rhett didn't even look up from the long shot he was making. "Probably a stack of citations and tickets. Winter's Edge isn't up to code, Striker. Too bad. You won't be having that grand opening you've been promoting after all."

"I haven't even heard of half of these, and you've revoked our liquor license the day before we open? Fucking really?"

"Tough luck, rogue. Maybe try opening your bar somewhere else. Like in Alaska. Perhaps I can't reach you there." Rhett moved around the table and took another shot, sinking the seven ball into the corner pocket. "Or maybe I can."

Tall and dangerous, Roman was shaking with fury, as if he might bolt for Rhett and snuff out his life right here in the dingy bar. Usually, Mila would've tried to calm him down to protect him from Rhett's revenge, but she was still on the high of residual fury, and the vision of Roman attacking that asshole was a pleasant thought.

It's going to be so fun to break you, Mila.

It would be fun to watch Roman break Rhett.

"Roman?" she asked.

His bright eyes drifted straight to her, and he nodded his chin.

"Are you still hiring at Winter's Edge?" God, she was going to do this. With trembling hands, she removed her Four Horsemen apron.

Roman's smile was two parts mischief, one part pride. He dragged his molten gaze to Rhett as he answered her, "I sure am. You want head bartender? I'll let you manage the whole bar."

Eyes on the ground, Mila clenched her hands at her sides, and as she passed the others, told Tim, "I quit. Seems I've found a better offer." By someone who would've never stood aside and let Rhett slam her against a wall.

"No," Rhett said blandly. "Get back to work, Mila, stop fucking around."

Roman's touch was light on her lower back as he guided her toward the door.

"Mila!" Rhett screamed like a psychopath.

She hunched and plugged her ears so she wouldn't hear the order she knew was coming. Roman cupped his big hands over her ears, too, and rushed her outside, slamming the door behind them. He didn't let them slow to celebrate but veered them straight toward his jeep, loaded up in a hurry, and then he peeled out of there, skidding across the black ice as he escaped the parking lot.

Heaving breath that fogged the window, she watched out the back window as Rhett ran across the parking lot after them. He opened his mouth and yelled, but the roar of Roman's engine drowned out the sound of his fury.

"What did you just do?" Roman asked, looking so proud she wanted to crow.

"I just stopped being the chicken. I think I want to be the big bad wolf now."

ELEVEN

Mila shouldn't be this excited about what she'd done, but the hope that had slowly begun blooming in her chest since the day Roman returned to Rangeley was now like a sunflower—wide open, stretching for the sky, catching the wind.

Her toothpaste fell off the counter in her hurry to pack, so she bent over and picked it up, then tossed it into the big, silver sparkly bag she'd gotten for free when she'd purchased enough bras at an online boutique. She was moving into ten-ten!! Okay, maybe not moving so much as staying there until the danger from Rhett blew over, but Roman had asked her on the way back to her place.

She stared at her reflection in the mirror and

canted her head. Her cheeks were rosy, her eyes bright. Always bright because of the magic Odine had used to bind her here. But she looked happy. Even alone in the bathroom, her lips were curved up in a faint smile, her natural expression now. On a whim, she pulled a couple of bobby pins out of the hand-thrown pot she'd made in high school that she kept on the counter, and then pinned her thick bangs back into her high ponytail. She'd curled her dark hair this morning, and as she studied herself in the mirror, she was taken aback by how very different she looked since Roman had come back home. Here was a peek at self-confidence, something she thought she'd lost forever on the day she'd pledged to the Bone-Rippers. She looked different with her bangs not hiding her eyes, but she kind of liked it. And Roman was always pushing them to the side. She hoped he liked her hair, too.

He was outside on the phone. She could hear the soft rumble of his voice, but couldn't make out his words. He was pissed at what Rhett was pulling to keep Winter's Edge closed, but Mila knew a few things about permits from helping Tim get the Four Horsemen up and running, and she was going to help the Strikers sort through the mess Rhett had made. It might not open as soon as they had hoped, but Mila swore on everything she owned that she was going to help them get the grand opening back on track. And then she was going to be the best bar manager ever. She'd worked at Winter's Edge when she'd come of age, and now it would be a homecoming.

Roman would be there. And Gentry, Asher, and Blaire.

No more getting bullied by the pack. No more Rhett. She didn't know how she was going to do it, but she was going to become a rogue like the people who were beginning to mean so much to her. She'd always thought being part of a pack was necessary for her submissive wolf, but right now, being part of a family felt much more important.

Shouldering the giant bag of clothes and toiletries, Mila made her way to the front door, her snow boots tromping across the floorboards with every bouncy step. She grabbed her heaviest jacket and pulled open the door.

Roman was in the middle of throwing a snowball. It blasted against a tree.

"Are you mad?"

"Hmm?" he asked, turning around. "Whoa, hottie with a body. Your hair looks sexy as fuck. I can see your eyes better! And, no, I'm not mad." He picked up another handful of snow and packed it. "Just playing a little catch with the old man." He chucked that ball in the same direction as the other.

Mila stared at the empty yard and pursed her lips. At least he had a sense of humor about seeing ghosts. Roman pulled his ringing phone out of his back pocket and answered, "What?" Roman held his arm out as Mila approached and pulled her tight against his side, kissed the top of her hair.

It sounded like Gentry's voice on the phone.

"Wait, Blaire did?" Roman asked, taking her bag from her shoulder. "Badass. When? Yeah… Okay, we're on our way. Save me the biggest one." Roman began walking to his jeep, leaving Mila to trail behind. "Don't be a hairy sack, Gentry. I have the biggest dick, I need the biggest seat… Shut up. I hate you, too. See you in ten minutes." Roman ended the call and tossed her a bright, white grin over his shoulder. "Blaire got her hands on three snow machines. You want to ride up into Hunter Cove Wildlife Sanctuary and Change with us?"

"We're going wolf up in the sanctuary?" she asked in a higher pitch than she'd intended. Gah, she hadn't done that in years! "Yes!"

"Good. Blaire feels like she needs to Change, but she wants us to have a day off from the stress of the bar opening. We can't do anything about the permits until tomorrow, so tonight"—he gave her a mischievous grin—"we ride. I'll let you drive so I can hold onto your boobs and press my dick against your butt."

Mila let off a giggle. "You're so romantic."

"Only with you."

Mila was taken with excitement and ran and jumped onto Roman's back. He laughed loud, an easy one that echoed through the neighborhood. He clamped his teeth onto her forearm and tossed her bag in the back.

"Careful! I have expensive make-up in there."

"Expensive? Woman, nowhere in Rangeley sells expensive anything."

"I shop online," she said primly as she slid from his back and in through the door he held open for her. "I had to get creative when I figured out I couldn't leave the area."

"Clever wolfie," he murmured as he closed the door, but he wore a frown as he jogged around the front of his Jeep.

"How long have you been bound here?" he asked as he turned the engine.

"Odine did it when I was twenty. She said I needed to stay here for you."

"What?"

Mila smiled as she pressed her fingertips in front of the heater vents. The air was still warm. "She said you would come back. As much as I dislike her, she was right. And I'm glad you came back, even if it's just for a little while."

Roman dragged her palm to the beard on his jaw and rasped it against her hand. "No more talk of leaving. Today is for fun."

"Okay," she whispered. She liked to pretend about forever, too.

Roman drove them to the mouth of the Hunter Cove Wildlife sanctuary. Asher was unloading snow machines from a trailer behind his truck. And off to the side, Blaire had her arms thrown around Gentry's shoulders and they were looking at each other like there was no one else in the world but them. It was such an intimate, beautiful moment. Did she and Roman look like that when they stared at each other?

"Ugh, that's us, isn't it? We look just like that when we're about to make out."

Mila laughed at how close he'd been to her own thoughts and linked her hand with his. "We should out-mush them today."

"Great. Great idea. I want to gross them out like they gross me out. Deal."

Roman got out, and as she gathered her jacket from the back, he opened her door and bowed gallantly. "Milady. I would like to cordially invite you to piggyback ride me on the front. Let's bump hips."

Mila stared. "Roman, I was kidding. I don't really want to gross people out."

"Fiiiine." But Roman was grinning so big now, the one she liked the most. It was the crooked smirk that said he was looking for trouble. "Here, let me." He yanked her red winter hat out of her hands and backed her up against his Jeep, then slid her hat on slowly and groaned erotically when it slipped into place.

"Stop," she said, trying to control her giggles.

He did the same with her gloves, but louder, and

now Asher was standing on top of the empty trailer with his hands on his hips and a disgusted look on his face. Gentry was sucking face with Blaire.

"What the fuck is going on?" Asher yelled, looking between the couples. "I'm already tempted to leave your asses here to walk back to the inn."

"He's so grumpy," Roman whispered.

"I can hear you!" Asher yelled, hopping from the trailer with animal-like grace.

Roman leaned into her and sucked hard on her neck, moaned a ridiculous sound. Mila was trapped between laughter and being turned on because he was working his way to hickey-ville.

One of the snow machines roared to life, and Asher took off on a trail through the woods. Roman muttered a curse and dragged her toward the empty one while Mila shrugged her arms into her jacket and tried to keep up.

Gripping her hips, he helped her onto the machine as Gentry and Blaire revved theirs and headed off behind Asher.

"Aaah," Mila said excitedly as Roman mounted behind her, standing. "Which buttons? I haven't ridden in forever!"

Roman got it running like a pro and, sat snug against her back as she guided them toward the trees. "You better keep up Big Bad Wolf."

Laughing like a maniac, Mila raced through the trees on the worn snowmobile trail behind the others. She could barely see Blaire's bright red jacket on the back of the machine in front of them. It was her beacon and kept her on the gas in desperation to keep up. The wind whipped at her bare cheeks, and they ducked branches as one, but she and Roman were laughing so much her abs were getting one helluva workout. God, she loved this. It tasted like freedom. The air was so crisp here without the fumes of cars and logging trucks in town. All that filled her senses was pine sap, earth, and fresh mountain air. And Roman. Whatever cologne he wore always filled her head. It always made her hyper aware of him. Or maybe that was just his presence. He commanded attention wherever he went, even if he was quiet.

She loved the feel of his hands on her waist, and anytime they slowed to take a steep curve in the trail, he kissed her on the neck, the side of the head, the shoulder… It wasn't for show either. The others were too far ahead. This was just because he liked giving her affection. Roman surprised her so much from the boy she'd known.

He had every reason to grow up hard and jaded, but though he was dangerous to others, and a badass, he was always tender and encouraging with her. Perfect match. He'd talked about her light making his shadows smaller, but his shadows gave her backbone. They gave her the grit she'd been missing before. She would've never stuck up for herself today without Roman encouraging her to own her wolf, own her life, take her pride back.

They blasted through a tree line and into a clearing with low-lying shrubs and brush. Already Gentry and Asher were zigzagging trails all through there, doing donuts, barely missing each other. Mila sped to join them, wearing a smile that matched the others'. Her heart was in her throat as she joined in the dance. They made tracks on every untouched stretches of snow in that clearing before Gentry pulled over and cut the engine to his machine. Blaire was holding her stomach, and her face looked pained.

When a snarl ripped out of her, her teeth were sharper, her face paler. Good. Maybe it would be a quick Change for her. Mila dragged her off the snow machine and told the boys, "Give us some privacy, yeah?"

Roman was already removing his shirt, and Gentry and Asher were kicking out of their boots. Gentry's eyes lingered on Blaire, but he nodded.

Blaire barely made it to the trees before she buckled in on herself. Crap. Mila had to rush to take off her scarf, winter hat, jacket, sweater. The jeans tripped her up. Her boots had to be unlaced first, and her pants were tight like leggings, but the White Wolf of Winter's Edge ripped out of Blaire's skin before she could get them off. The wolf fell hard, turned around, and snapped at Mila, but she understood. There was fear in the white wolf's eyes. She'd almost died, almost been snuffed out of existence, and this was her first time claiming the body again. Mila's wolf was scared all the time after the black magic, so Blaire's experience would've traumatized her. Mila exposed her neck and sat there in the middle of the pile of clothes, waiting for Blaire to attack. She didn't, though. A few seconds later, there was a whine and then a soft lick on Mila's cheek.

She huffed a sigh of relief and began undressing herself. Her Change was fast, only a moment of blinding agony before she was fully furred and four-legged. She shook out her fur. She was much smaller than Blaire's wolf, but that was okay. Blaire wasn't making her feel that familiar stomach ache that dominants often did when they were trying to put her in her place. In fact, Blaire was pacing toward the clearing and back, bushy white tail swishing in a slow wag, tongue lolled out to the side. She yipped, but it turned into a sound like a yodel, and then to a hoarse howl.

That sound dragged a howl from Mila's throat, too. She couldn't stop herself even if she tried. And really, she didn't want to. The Striker's joined, and there was Roman's voice. God, she loved it. She'd been so happy the first time she'd heard it again, the night the Bone-Rippers had gone after Gentry and Blaire. When he and Asher had gone to howling, calling out the pack, calling them to war, she'd drawn up, frozen, unable to move because she was terrified and so damn happy all at once. She'd just known Roman would help fix what Rhett was doing to Rangeley.

His howl was her sanctuary.

Mila let the note die slowly in her throat, and then

there was a loaded moment where she locked gazes with Blaire before they took off at a dead run for the boys.

Roman was there, his gray and brown wolf massive, his eyes blazing gold, his chest deep like a barrel, and his front end muscular. His tail was curved up, and he held his head high. She lowered to her belly and wagged her tail in greeting as she scooted across the snow to him. Roman made a sneezing noise that made her want to laugh if she had the ability. She made it to his front paws at last and rolled over on her back, tongue hanging out in a wolfish grin. *Hi, boyfriend.*

Roman lowered to his chest in the snow like he wanted to play, and he snuffled his nose loudly against the scruff of her neck. Suddenly, he took off, but skidded to a stop ten yards away, circled back, and stared at her with his head cocked. Now it was Mila who was excitedly yipping because she could see the others behind him. Gentry's charcoal gray wolf with Blaire stumbling around him like she was either drunk on happiness or trying to remember how to use her animal body. Through the trees stood an enormous black wolf with eyes such a light silver they looked white. His hackles were raised, making him look aggressive, and his head was lowered, eyes locked on hers. Asher looked terrifying now, unlike when he was a kid. His wolf had always been dark, but more chocolate brown than black. And his eyes hadn't been so light, or his body so huge. And he'd never, ever felt this heavy. Already the weight of him pressed against her shoulders. Roman was one of the most dominant wolves she'd ever encountered, but Asher was a monster like the legendary werewolves. As if he could hear her thoughts, he peeled back his black lips over bright white, razor sharp teeth and snarled a terrifying sound. That was impossible, though. Still, she was going to stick like glue to her mate. Roman would protect her from the demon wolf.

Blaire looked up suddenly, and Mila followed her gaze to a single fat snowflake that drifted slowly toward the ground. Another touched Mila's ear, and she twitched it to get rid of the itch. And suddenly, the gray clouds above opened up with the gentle snow. Blaire went nuts, running around so fast her butt was tucked under her as she ducked and dodged the snowflakes. Mila wanted to play, so she ran after her, chasing her around in zigzags through the trees until the boys trotted off toward the sharp incline that led up the mountain. Mila loved everything about today!

She and Blaire took off after the Strikers, and Mila nipped at Roman's back leg when she passed. He went from a trot to a sprint and chased her. When he caught her, she wasn't even afraid, just happy. Happy, happy, happy. No one in this mismatched rogue family would hurt her. Except for maybe Asher. She did not want to play with him. And he seemed to feel the same because he ignored all their antics and trotted steadily upward, as if he didn't care if they followed or not. Gentry was ducking in and out now, nipping at them, biting Roman, wrestling too hard, so Mila and Blaire disengaged from the wolf fight and loped beside each other through the trees, snapping at the snowflakes, and giving big wolf grins whenever they caught one.

Roman and Gentry were snarling loudly behind them, ripping each other up and down the hill, but they wouldn't kill each other. Probably. Still, Mila skidded to a stop and waited for them to stop bleeding each other. Asher had disappeared into the thick brush up the hill, but she could trail him just fine. His scent, his dominance, and the fresh wolf tracks in the snow were all easy to follow, like a map. Roman joined her again, his ear and leg bleeding, but otherwise he seemed fine. Crazy boys, always brawling like that. Blaire was licking a bite mark on the side of Gentry's face. It looked awful but would probably heal by tomorrow.

The others took off like a shot, and Mila barked and took off, too. She didn't sense the dark magic until she'd blasted into the invisible barrier. She was flung backward, and with a yelp of pain, she slid on her side through the snow with the force of it.

Roman was right there, whining, his nose buried against her ribs, her neck, her ear. Mila felt sick from the dump of magic into her system. Stupid Odine. This was as far as she could go. Mila's disappointment was infinite. Roman cast a quick glance to where the others had disappeared, but when he looked back at her, his eyes were softer. Sympathetic. He nudged her upward and trotted back down the trail. Feeling gutted, she followed him, her tail tucked between her legs. When the others came out of the brush toward the west ten minutes later, Mila felt even worse. Her being bound to this territory by Odine meant she was changing the course of their adventure today.

Roman was playing, ducking in and out, nipping at her, encouraging her to run with him. She knew he was just trying to make her feel better, but it wouldn't work. Not right now. This was supposed to be a fun day of running the wildlife sanctuary with her friends, not thinking about the grit that had overtaken her life. She was holding Roman back.

She would always hold him back.

It wasn't fair.

Roman was her freedom, but she was a snare, one that would wrap tighter and tighter around his throat the longer he stayed.

Love wasn't supposed to be like that. It wasn't shackles and traps. It wasn't pulling the man who cared for her into quicksand along with her just to avoid the loneliness while she sank.

Mila wanted the world for herself, but something had changed within her over the last few weeks.

Now, she also wanted the world for Roman.

TWELVE

Mila startled awake, and for a moment, couldn't remember where she was. This place smelled so familiar, but it wasn't home.

She was in ten-ten with Roman. It was so dark she had to blink several times to try to adjust her vision to the room. There was a dark figure standing at the end of the bed. Roman.

Mila sat up slowly and rubbed her eyes, then squinted into the darkness. "What's wrong?"

"He won't answer you," Roman said from behind her. He was standing in the open doorway with a half empty glass of water in his hands. He wore nothing but a pair of teal briefs and a frown.

Chills rippled up her arms as she dragged her

gaze back to the figure standing at the end of the bed. It wasn't Roman at all, but someone who looked like him. Someone who had Roman's face and eyes. It was Noah.

"H-how can I see him?"

"I told you. I didn't want my darkness rubbing off on you. The longer you're with me, the worse it'll get." His teeth flashed white in the dark in a quick snarl. "I'm poison."

"Come here," she whispered, daring to give her back to the ghost.

Roman pushed off the frame and sauntered over to the bed, then sat down, much too far away from her. Mila crawled over to him and straddled his lap, wrapped her arms around his shoulders, and buried her face in his neck. He smelled stressed, and there was a soft growl rattling his throat. Mila pressed her fingertips against the vibration. "Why?"

"Because I don't like him this close to you. Because I'm angry that you can see him. Because I'm still angry at him. Asher and Gentry got to escape. They got closure. Dump the ashes, they're done. I get to see him everywhere. I get to remember how it was. He wears the same dead look he used to give me when I was a kid. I get to see it for eternity."

Mila kissed his neck gently, then sucked, licked him softly, sucked, rolled her hips against his. "Can you see him now?" she whispered against his skin.

Roman turned his head toward where Noah had stood. "No. Can you?"

Mila eased away enough to scan the room and shook her head. "No." Thank God. She'd never seen a ghost before and gooseflesh still covered her body.

Roman rubbed his warm hands up and down her arms. "You don't have to be scared. They never do anything. They're just there. Especially in Rangeley. Something about this place makes it worse."

Mila's heart hurt so bad because, in this moment, she knew she would never ask him to become her alpha. She was stuck here, but if Roman was stuck here with her, he would be tortured by the ghost of his father, and whatever else he saw that often made his eyes go vacant. Roman was hers, but not for always, and something about that slashed poignant pain through her chest, as if her heart were being ripped from the cavity and handed to Roman. He would hold it gently while he was here in their hometown, she knew he would, but when he left, he would take her heart with him, and she would be left to always walk this earth empty, just like the ghosts.

Her eyes prickled with tears, and she squeezed them tightly closed to keep them inside. Swimming in her pain, she kissed him, soft lips on soft lips.

"What's wrong?" he murmured cupping her cheeks and pushing her back so he could look into her eyes. His were glowing gold.

"Nothing."

"Lie. I swear the ghosts won't hurt you, Mila. I wouldn't let anything hurt you."

"Can we…can we just get lost for a while? In each other?" She wanted to forget about the hurt and just enjoy the time she did have with Roman. Her Roman.

With a wicked smile, he said, "Woman, I can't get lost in you. Your pussy is as tight as a—"

"Roman!"

"It's like the size of a pencil sharpener," he muttered, easing her onto her back on the mattress. "I barely fit. I mean, it feels good, but damn you must've had some little-dicked boyfriends before I came along."

Mila covered her blazing cheeks with her hands. "None of this is appropriate talk if you are trying to seduce me."

Roman snorted. "I don't have to try. You smell like you want sex every time I look at you."

"I do not! Oooooh," she moaned as he buried his face between her legs. Mila gripped his hair and rocked her hips upward.

The little teaser, Roman was kissing her gently, one inner thigh, and the other, then right at her clit, then back to the thighs, his beard scratching her sensitive skin. And with each pass, he clamped down a little harder. When he ran his tongue up her slit, she was done for, begging him for more, rolling her hips toward him in desperation.

She spread her knees wider and arched her back as Roman plunged his tongue deep inside her. How was he so good at this? He sucked on her clit and slid into her again and again until she was boneless, mindless...until nothing existed except for the body-shattering sensation of his tongue pleasing and teasing her. She was right on the edge, right there, right on the verge when he lifted up and pulled himself up her body and slid his dick into her in one smooth motion. His teeth were on her neck, and all Mila could do as he gave her thrust after controlled, deep thrust was cradle his head, nails in his scalp. She moaned each time they connected at the hips.

He clamped down, hard, but not hard enough to break her skin, and she wanted to beg him to do it. *Bite her.* But she couldn't risk it, couldn't risk him becoming her alpha, couldn't risk her wolf bonding to his, so she stayed quiet. Her body was on fire where he touched her. His hard chest and abs flexed as he bucked into her. Teeth on her sensitive neck, his beard rasping against her skin, his cock so big he stretched her with every entry. Roman pulled her knee up, drove deeper, and she was done. Orgasm blasted through her, and she cried out mindlessly. Teeth, teeth. Please. Please no. Please yes.

Roman pushed into her so deep she gasped at the shock of it. He huffed a groan and spilled warmth into her, reared back, and did it again and again. "I love you," he ground out as he slowed. "Fuck. I should've waited. I love you."

Roman eased up. There was no smile, no joking on his face. Just gold, serious eyes that beheld her like she was beautiful. Like she was everything. A tear slid from the corner of her eye, but Roman leaned over and licked it with the tip of his tongue. With anyone else, that would've been strange, but not with him. Roman wasn't like other men. He wasn't even like other werewolves. He was more. Never had he made her feel ashamed of her submissiveness, her body. Never had he made her feel weak. And now he was cleaning her tears the way his animal demanded, and she adored him for it. Adored him, adored his wolf. They were both hers.

Roman's hand slipped gently behind her neck. He lifted her chin up as he pressed his lips to hers. There was no rush to disconnect, no hurry to leave her in bed. He seemed to only want to touch her, and now she wanted to cry harder. He loved her? He loved her.

Mila slid her hand to his wrist to hold his touch at the back of her neck, and she parted her lips slightly to allow his tongue inside. Shallow strokes. He brushed his tongue against hers like he was tasting something for the first time. Maybe minutes passed. Maybe hours. Time meant nothing when she was all tangled up with him like this. When at last Roman pecked her with a soft smack and rolled them to their sides, facing each other, the gold had faded from his eyes. They stayed like that, lost in each other's gazes as the early dawn light filtered through the bedroom window. It felt as if they were speaking without words. She fancied she could see his soul in the sky blue of his eyes, and maybe he could see hers, too. Their legs were tangled, and their fingers explored the lines of each other's bodies. Mila memorized him. The tattoos she would trace later when she wasn't lost in the blue, but she had the feel of him, of his musculature, the exact texture of his skin, his scent, everything committed to memory that she would hold onto for always.

"Roman?" she said on a breath, at last breaking the beautiful silence.

He lifted her knuckles to his lips and smiled as he laid a gentle kiss there. "I know. I can feel it."

"But I want to say it."

He pulled her hand to his chest, right over his heart. "Feel what happens when you do."

She offered him a slow smile and splayed her hand against his chest. "I love you, too."

His heart thumped harder, faster, and her smile stretched wider across her face. He watched her lips with awe in his eyes. It felt so good to smile this much now. Roman had done that for her. He'd given her happiness again. He'd given her hope.

Even if that hope was going to end up destroying her, it was worth it for this moment right here.

Roman's smile dipped from his face, and his eyes jerked to the window, his body instantly tense.

"What is it?" she asked, but now she could hear it, too. Or perhaps she could *feel* the rumble of the truck engine. It was so faint, but familiar, and dread dumped into her system.

Roman snarled and slid from bed. She did the same in a panic and began searching for her clothes as Roman flipped the light on.

They were both dressed by the first flash of blue and red lights. Roman didn't say a word, only pulled her jacket from the coat rack and held it open for her to slide her arms into. He was strung as tight as a bow string and smelled of fury. It was hard to meet his gaze. Her wolf wanted to run from him and be closer to him at the same time. A whine worked its way up her throat, but Roman kissed her forehead and settled the sound. And then he took her hand and pulled her behind him to meet the trouble that was parking in the snowy lot in a big police truck, flanked by two cruisers. Rhett had brought the humans on his force. Fuck.

Across the parking lot, Gentry and Blaire were running toward ten-ten, and Asher was jogging down his porch steps toward them, clad in a pair of gray sweatpants and no shirt.

Rhett got out of his truck with a vile grin on his face, his eyes flashing too bright. Mila snarled as he strode up to the porch. That was a new reaction, and it startled her enough to make her jump and squeeze onto Roman's hand tighter behind his back.

"What do you want?" Roman ground out.

Rhett rested a boot on the bottom step and twirled a pair of handcuffs around his index finger. "You're under arrest for the murder of Hal Dunmar."

"Who?" Roman asked.

"The hunter you killed in the woods."

Roman glanced up at the porch rafters with a humorless huff of breath and then back to Rhett. "You've got to be fucking kidding me. You're gonna pin your kill on me?"

Fury flashed through Rhett's eyes, and he looked back at the two human officers approaching. Before they were within hearing range, he looked right at Roman and snarled his lip up before he said, "I sure am. Told you to stay away from her." He straightened his spine and smiled brightly. And then he began reading Roman his rights as Rhett made his way up the stairs.

"No, no, no, you can't arrest him," Mila said, maneuvering between Roman and Rhett. "He didn't do anything."

"He murdered a hunter in cold blood, Mila. He needs to be punished."

"You did that—"

"Stop talking." Power blasted through Rhett's words, and Mila choked on her argument. Every time she tried to get a word out, it stole her breath away.

"What's going on?" Gentry asked.

The police officer closest to the middle Striker brother strong-armed him in the chest. "Stay back. All of you, stay back." He jammed a finger at Blaire and Asher. "Back off."

Asher promptly ignored him and shoved right through him. And then he pushed through the other one, too, as Roman told Rhett, "Stop that fucking order. She can't breathe."

"She could if she stopped talking!" Rhett was letting his control slip in front of his deputies. "I don't know how she's here with you right now, I don't know what you've done to her, but you'll pay for that, too. There are rules, Mila!" he screamed in her face, his cheeks going red and veins popping out of his neck.

Roman hit him so fast she barely had time to get out of the way. They went to the ground, but Rhett hadn't been prepared for Roman's fury and ended up on bottom with Roman holding his shirt and blasting him across the jaw over and over in a blur.

Mila rushed forward, but Asher was already there pulling his brother off Rhett, who was now laughing like a maniac. "Assaulting a police officer. I knew you were stupid, Striker, but not that stupid."

Roman lunged at him again, but Asher held him back and demanded, "Stop it, Roman. It won't help anything. He's baiting you. Stop!" That last word had heavy power to it, like Rhett's words. They had the same effect on Roman, too, because he stopped struggling and looked like he was about to go to his knees. With a grunt, he exposed his neck to the eldest Striker brother, whose eyes were way too light right now and whose face was snarled up like a demon's. Asher was telling Roman something with his eyes, some warning, and when he closed and reopened them again, they were human blue instead of wolf silver. The amount of control over the wolf it must have taken to do that made Mila draw up and realize she didn't know Asher anymore. But she knew enough to be frightened of him.

Gentry and Blaire were up on the porch now, standing beside Asher and Roman, and Mila stepped forward beside her mate. She shook like a leaf and couldn't lift her eyes from the ground as Rhett stood up, but she didn't back down either, and that was something big for her.

Roman made her feel stronger.

The three police officers stood across the porch, Rhett at the helm, furious eyes zeroed in on Roman. "Get in the fucking truck, Striker, or I'll have every precinct within a fifty-mile radius here to watch you resist arrest. We'll just add it to your pile of fuck-ups."

Roman's chest was heaving, and he made the air feel heavy, but when he looked down at Mila, his eyes were softer. "Stay here with Gentry and Asher."

"No, Roman, you can't. You didn't do anything wrong!"

"Stay here where it's safe. They'll keep you protected," he murmured as he stepped toward

Rhett.

Rhett was too rough on him putting on the handcuffs, and Mila rushed him, ready to rip his throat out. "I hate you!" she screamed as Asher caught her by the waist and settled her near Blaire. Again and again, Mila tried to get to Rhett, but Blaire was helping hold her back now, too. Mila sobbed. "Why can't you just let me have one thing?" she asked Rhett. "Why can't I have anything! Why do you have to keep me unhappy?"

"Because you're mine!" Rhett screamed, voice echoing through the hills.

"What?" Jake, one of the human officers, asked. He was frowning and was looking from face to face. "Rhett, what's going on. Mila don't belong to anyone."

"Get in your car," Rhett ground out, shoving Roman down the stairs so hard he barely stayed upright.

Roman had his head down, but his muscles strained against his thin T-shirt, and his frozen breath chugged in front of him. As he was pushed into the back of the truck, one flash of his blinding gold eyes said he could very well be found out at the precinct. Shit.

Mila shoved away from Asher and chased the police cars that peeled out of the lot. "We have to do something!" she sobbed, wrapping her arms around her stomach in an attempt to keep from breaking apart. Her wolf howled to rip out of her and chase them.

"We'll have to talk to Terry Grant. He was dad's lawyer. He'll know what to do," Asher said in a gruff voice, his eyes on the disappearing headlights.

"You don't understand," Mila said, warm tears streaking down her cheeks. "This is what happened to the pack members who disappeared. Rhett would pin something awful on them, and we would never see them again. And Asher, I've been searching for them. They aren't in the prison systems. They're just...*gone!*" Her breath hitched as she ripped her gaze away from the shock on the Strikers' faces and watched the cars disappear behind the snow-covered trees.

Now Roman—her Roman—was gone, too.

THIRTEEN

In the driver's seat, Rhett wiped the blood from his split lip with the back of his hand. The movement made his collar shift to the side to show the red, angry scars where Gentry had damn near beheaded Rhett the night they'd come for him and Blaire. It looked awful, like his shifter healing wasn't working. Good. Roman hoped the pain kept him up at nights.

"You smell sick," Roman observed as he leaned back as well as he could with his hands cuffed painfully behind him. "You smell *weak*. Must be hard to hold the pack like that."

"I'm holding the pack just fine, Striker. And most importantly of all, Mila. Did you see her bow to my command? While you rot in jail, I'll be fucking her relentlessly. You've caused some problems with obedience, but I'll bring my alpha female back around. I'll fix her."

Fury pounded through Roman's veins, and the edges of his vision tinted red. He closed his eyes and tried to focus on steadying his breathing. *Inhale, exhale, don't kill that mother fucker.* How tempting it was to blast through the glass that separated them and finish Rhett with nothing but his teeth. But Asher was right. Rhett had baited him by getting in Mila's face, and Roman had lost it. Lost control. Lost his mind with the instinct to protect her. He'd given them more reason to arrest him.

"I have big plans for you, Striker. I thought I would sell Gentry first, but you've earned my hate so much more. You tainted Mila, and because of that, I'm going to ruin your entire life. I'm going to make you wish you'd never laid eyes on her. It'll be a brutal death for you. One that makes you hate every breath you breathe and beg for the end."

Sell Gentry? Roman narrowed his eyes at the back of Rhett's head. What the fuck was he talking about?

He'd never been afraid of death. The ghosts around him made him realize things about death that others didn't understand. Death wasn't the end. It was just a pit stop to something different. But now he had Mila, and suddenly, the thought of dying was unacceptable. Not for him. But because, as long as Mila lived, he wanted to be here to protect her always.

"Why did you kill that hunter, Rhett?"

"Because he was nosey, because I saw him setting a wolf-trap in my territory, and because it was fun. And if you're trying to get me to confess on camera," he gritted out, pointing at the mounted lens on the front window, "the audio doesn't work. I'm a smarter wolf than you in every way, Striker. Always was. You were jokes. You were the dumb jock all the girls fell over themselves to fuck. I was the one in the shadows, working the pack like a chess game until I could take the throne."

"Steal the throne," Roman ground out. "Don't pretend you won alpha in a challenge, you fucking vermin. I know you murdered my dad, human, in the woods, like a fucking coward."

"Bottom Bitch has been talking about things she was ordered not to."

"Well, I guess that means she's not your Bottom

Bitch. You're losing control of your chess pieces, Rhett. Can you feel us? I wonder if you could feel us breathing down the back of your neck. Gentry would love nothing more than to finish that rip-job on your throat. I've never seen Asher care about a person one way or the other, but when we talk about you, he looks like a fucking blood-thirsty demon. Blaire, Odine, Mila...and then there's me, Rhett. I won't be forgetting the shit you've done to this town, to my family, to my mate—"

"My mate!"

Roman smiled because he couldn't help himself. Who was easily riled up now? Rhett was like a spoiled child with a bag of candy he couldn't finish but didn't want to share. Tantrums when someone threatened to take it away.

Rhett spun his tires and skidded across a lane as he turned too sharply into the small police station at the edge of town. Red had crept up his neck, and even his ears were the color of cherries now. So angry. Roman had a temper, too, but right now he was checking Rhett for weaknesses.

Rhett locked up the brakes as he skidded into a parking spot, then pulled out his phone. He connected a call. "I've got another one for you. A big one. Brawler. Dominant. When can you come get him?" Rhett stared out the side window and waved off one of the deputies that was approaching the truck. "I don't fuckin' know, Anderson. You asked for a big one. I'm delivering. He's one of the Strikers... Yeah, the mother fuckin' Strikers, Noah's bloodline... Are you serious right now? I'm telling you I have a Striker, and you're telling me you can't get him until the morning? I'm not sitting on him for an entire night! Come get him, or I'll be bringing him to you myself. And trust me when I say you don't want me inconvenienced right now. I want a bigger cut, too... Nope. Higher." Rhett snarled loudly into the phone. A few seconds later, he gritted out, "Better. I'll see you tonight."

Whatever this was, it wasn't about locking Roman up for that hunter's death. It wasn't about ruining his record, or dragging this out in trial. Rhett was dumb, but not dumb enough to send a werewolf to prison. The first Change behind bars would out their entire species. No, Roman wouldn't be shipped off to prison. Rhett was doing something awful. Selling wolves? For what?

Roman stared out the window, his thoughts racing. He could break out of here with little effort, but he was right on the cusp of what Rhett had really been doing to the pack and to the town. If he ran, he'd look guilty of killing that hunter, but worse than that, he'd have to leave Mila. She was bound, and he would be on the lam.

And right now, he didn't want to run. He wanted to see this through. He wanted to gather every bit of ammunition he could against Rhett and destroy not only him, but any legacy of terror he'd left in Rangeley. The wolf inside of him was so curious to what was actually going on here he couldn't move to break the glass even if he tried.

He had to know. Even if it hurt, he had to find out why Dad had been killed, why the pack had rolled over for Rhett, why Mila was so scared of the people she used to consider friends.

The Wolves of Winter's Edge couldn't fix this town unless Roman found out what was really going on here.

FOURTEEN

"Two days." Mila glared at Nick, the officer at the front desk. "Two days, and you won't even let me see him? It's not right. He didn't do anything wrong!"

"Mila, I understand you're upset," he said low, a warning flashing in his eyes. "But I can't let you back there." He lowered his voice to a whisper. "It's not up to me on this one."

"Then I'll wait," Mila said, voice shaking. Gentry and Asher were outside, but they'd told her to make it happen this time, no matter what. She was the only one who knew Nick and the other officers in this town. She had the rapport, and Nick had shut down the Strikers hard when they'd tried to visit Roman. It was on her to make sure Roman was okay in here.

Stubbornly, she plopped down in one of the two black, plastic chairs against the wall, directly across from Nick's desk. Mila narrowed her eyes at him. She was fully prepared to pull this staring contest for the next dozen hours if she had to.

Nick tried to work for a while, but she could tell he was uncomfortable under her gaze. Felt nice. Usually she couldn't hold her gaze on anything without having to look at the floor, but things had been a-changin' since Roman had blown into town and turned her world upside down. Now she was pissed, scared for him, and protective as hell over the man she'd adored all those years ago and now loved deeply.

"I'm thirsty," she announced.

Nick was filling out paperwork, but at her complaint, he rolled his eyes closed in irritation and sighed heavily. "Do you want some water?"

"Yes."

"Then get some." He gestured to the blue jug on the stand. There were paper cone cups, but the jug was empty. She'd made sure before she mentioned being thirsty.

"I would if there was any water in there. My

throat is parched." She coughed delicately, but Nick narrowed his eyes. Perhaps that was going too far above her acting ability, so she swallowed it down and huffed a sigh. "Shall I eat some snow then?" she asked testily.

"Dammit, Mila," he muttered as he stood and strode down a hallway and out of sight. She could hear him returning in a rush, though, so she feigned boredom as he peeked his head around the corner. "Don't move." And then he disappeared down the hallway again.

That little command would've worked if he was her alpha, but Nick was human, and she wasn't in the mood to mind rules right now. Not after two mother-freaking days of worrying senseless about Roman rotting in that jail cell.

Mila bolted for the desk she'd seen him put his keys, grabbed the ring, then ran for the door at the back of the room. There were at least a dozen keys, but she got it on the third and sprinted down a long hallway to a trio of cells at the end. All were empty. Empty, empty, empty. Mila paced, running her fingers through her hair and gripping her locks. Where the fuck was he?

"Hey!" Nick yelled from down the hallway. "You can't be back there."

"He's not even here! Nick, what the fuck? Where is he?"

Nick was jogging toward her, but he didn't look mad. He looked worried, and when he got close enough, she could smell it—the bitter scent of fear.

"Mila, you have to leave. Rhett will be back soon—"

"Nick, you know me. You've known me for a long time. I'm a good person, an honest one, and I'm telling you, Roman had nothing to do with that hunter's death."

"I know," Nick said on a breath. He scanned the hallway behind him and gripped her shoulders. "Mila, I know. I know what you are, what Roman is, what half the damn town is. Rhett...he's not careful. Someone in a black SUV came and picked up Roman a few hours after he was brought in. I have no idea where he is and have no way of finding out. Rhett told us not to talk about it. Everything is so— Mila, I have a family."

"Stop. I don't want to hear it, Nick. Roman is my family, and now he's God-knows-where, and you covered for that monster."

She shoved past him, bumping his shoulder hard. Mila's eyes burned with tears, but she blinked them back because they were out of time. If Roman was still alive…

God, she couldn't think like that. He was. He was still alive. She just had to figure out how to find him. Her heart was drumming hard against her sternum as she shoved the door open. The cold winter wind hit her face and stole her breath away. The boys were waiting by Asher's truck, leaned on the bed, arms crossed, but the second she hit the sidewalk and started jogging toward them, they shoved off Asher's ride and both muttered curses, as if they could tell from the panic on her face what had happened.

"He's not in there. He's not in there!"

"Shhh," Gentry said, hugging her up tight.

She felt trapped, though. These weren't the arms she wanted. They weren't the ones that would tell her with an embrace everything would be okay. Everything was not okay! She eased back and paced, shaking her hands out as she tried to think. "Nick said a black SUV picked Roman up a few hours after he arrived here. That means he's been out of Rangeley for two days. Two days!"

Asher was a stone. The only thing that moved were his eyes as he tracked her progress back and forth over the empty parking spot. "I think it's time to see Odine."

"Whaaat the fuck, Asher?" Gentry asked. "No. We need to find Roman, not play with whatever evil she's wielding."

"Yeah, we need to find Roman." Asher jammed a finger at Mila. "But she's stuck, Gentry. And Odine knows shit we don't."

His phone chirped, and chills blasted up Mila's spine when Asher checked the caller ID and gave a dark laugh. "Odine says we need to see her right now. Get in the truck."

Gentry locked eyes with Mila as Asher got behind the wheel.

"Get in!" Asher barked, and those two simple words forced her legs to move. It shouldn't have. Asher wasn't her alpha, but Gentry was making his way to the back seat of the truck, jerking with each step, as if he had no control either.

Mila scrambled into the passenger's seat and slammed the door beside her. "I don't know what's wrong with you, or what's wrong with your wolf, Asher, but I'm not your pack. Gentry either. You need to cut the orders out."

"I didn't mean to," he snarled as he spun out of the parking lot. "I forget that..."

"Forget what?" Gentry asked softly from the back seat.

Asher scrubbed his hand down his blond facial scruff. "I forget I can do that."

"*Why* can you do that?" Mila asked carefully.

Asher reached forward and turned up the volume on the radio instead of answering. He felt way too heavy, so Mila cracked the window to get some fresh air, and then she pressed herself as far away from Asher as possible, where she stayed flat as a pancake for the duration of the fifteen-minute drive out to Odine's cabin.

Odine was waiting on the front porch, wrapped in a thick blanket, and smoking a pipe. Her olive skin was leathered, and there was more gray in her hair than Mila remembered. Her jet-black eyes looked exhausted. When they got out, the witch didn't say a word, only gestured them inside. Mila stepped into the dim entryway, but when Asher and Gentry tried to follow, Odine held up her hand and told them, "Not you, boys. Just her."

"Wait," Mila said, panicked as she bolted for the open door. It slammed closed before she could reach it.

The last time she'd been inside Odine's house, she'd been bound to Rangeley. Three days of torture, nightmares, hovering in the in-between, and convinced she would die at any moment. Mila was too terrified to turn around. She'd only come in here because she thought Gentry and Asher would be with her. Being alone with the witch wasn't something she'd been mentally prepared for, and now she was frozen, too afraid to even breathe.

"I told you when I did the binding that Roman would need you. Mila, you were going to leave. I could see it coming. You weren't going to stay around Rangeley forever, and I needed you here when Roman came back."

"Why?"

"Because you can heal him. You can save him. You can banish the ghosts he sees. You can give him a life I always wanted for him. No one else on this earth can do that. Just you. He needs you now."

"Do you know where he is?"

"In darkness. No exact location, just...glimpses. But Asher's starting to figure it out. The dark wolf can get you close, but you'll be the one who has to save him, Mila. Do you understand?"

"No! You're talking in riddles like you always do!"

Odine began to chant something low behind her, and when Mila slowly turned around, Odine was standing in the small, cluttered kitchen, holding the same bouquet of herbs she'd used to bind her to Rangeley. Mila could tell from the awful smell. She would never forget that scent as long as she lived. Her wolf revolted in fear, and Mila cried out at the pain of the Change and dropped to her knees.

"No, girl, not here and not now," Odine said, clawing her fingers of her empty hand like she was gripping an invisible ball. A glowing, lavender spark erupted there.

Mila gasped at the searing pain in her chest. It felt like the witch had shoved her hand into her ribcage and was holding her heart, squeezing it. The Change stopped, and Mila threw her head back in agony. Her body was moving, rising. Her knees lifted from the floor, and then her dragging feet did, too. She was levitating up near the rafters of the low ceiling, her hands out, terror clogging her throat as the witch's eyes turned completely black. The chanting got louder, filling Mila's head, the words echoing and overlapping each other until it was just a low humming sound that vibrated through her body.

She was taking something from Mila. Mila could see the pulsing black fog drifting from her skin. It floated toward Odine, and the woman absorbed it. Was she taking her essence? Her life? Her years? Her wolf?

Mila was so scared she tried to cry out for help, but the second she got the word "Asher" past her vocal cords, she slammed back to the wooden floor. Mila gasped deeply, dragging precious oxygen into her lungs. Her body hurt. She felt like her skin had been ripped off her and her innards set on fire. It hurt so bad she couldn't see straight, couldn't do anything but crawl pathetically with no destination in mind.

Across the room, Odine sat hard into a chair and buried her face in her hands. She was heaving breath like Mila was. But at the first hitch in that breath, Mila realized she was crying.

The pain was fading, becoming more bearable.

"What did you do?" she rasped out.

In a hoarse voice, like she hadn't used it in days, Odine croaked out, "You can go now."

"W-what?"

"I want you to go now. I want you to bring him back."

"I can leave Rangeley?" Mila asked, too afraid to hope.

Odine pulled her face from her hands. Her cheeks were smeared with tears, and she looked heartbroken. "I can't lose another, you understand? After Noah..." Odine swallowed hard a few times before she tried again. "Call the white wolf. You'll need clothes."

"What kind of clothes?"

"Something sexy. Ripped up. Gritty. Where you're going...you can't look innocent. The monsters would eat you alive. Dress like you are a monster, too. Now go. You're running out of time. I can feel him—" Odine shook her head and winced. "This is your moment, Mila. The one your life has built up to. Don't waste it."

Baffled, Mila stood and made her way to the door. She turned, feeling like she should thank Odine for something, but she didn't understand what. "I'll see you later," she said instead.

Odine gave a sad smile. "I hope so."

Mila frowned and then made her way down the steps. The door slammed closed behind her, but she could hear Odine crying again inside as she made her way toward Asher's truck. Her skin was tingling, and she smelled different. She didn't have that faint black magic smell anymore. Any other time, she would've celebrated. She would've jumped up and run around in circles laughing and crowing, but right now, all she cared about was hitting that county line, moving past it, and finding Roman. Odine was scared for him, and for some reason, that terrified Mila.

"Are you okay?" Gentry asked, his bright green eyes wide as he studied her face.

"I think so." But she wouldn't be if they didn't get to Roman. "He's running out of time. That's what Odine said."

Asher was staring at his phone with a frown. "Rhett's on the move."

"What?" Gentry asked.

"I put a tracker in his truck the day I came back here. He hasn't left town this entire time, but right now, he's headed north." He inhaled deeply and locked his eerie silver gaze on Mila. "You know him best, Mila. If Rhett was going to end Roman, what would he do?"

Dread spread through her body like corpse fingers unfurling. "He would want to watch."

Asher nodded, wholly unsurprised. "We need to follow him."

"Yeah," she said, running around the front of the truck, "but first I have to call Blaire."

"Why?" Gentry asked as he loaded up in the back.

"Because I need a change of clothes."

Mila had always hated Odine for what she'd done to her, but she couldn't deny the witch knew things beyond the realm of reason. That, and she had some tender spot in her black heart for Roman. She'd said Mila needed to match the monsters they would find, so okay.

She didn't like it, but tonight, Mila was going to trust the witch.

FIFTEEN

The floor of his cell was stained dark and smelled of iron. Roman winced and grabbed his ribs as if that would ease the pain of the broken one. The last two days had been hell, and his shifter healing was slowing down. Not a good sign.

Bright side—he knew exactly what kind of animal Rhett was now. He was dealing werewolves, selling his own people to dog fights. Bad news, though— Roman was having trouble figuring out how to save himself from this. And if he didn't survive another night, it wouldn't make any difference how much he'd learned over the last forty-eight hours.

He swallowed a groan of pain as he wrapped his battered knuckles with tape. There weren't many rules, but no gloves were allowed. The paying customers wanted a blood-bath. The crowd loved when one of the contenders was opened up.

Beside him, a dappled black and gray wolf paced the cell length. Dirty metal bars separated them. The wolf, Hays, everyone called him, wouldn't last through the fights tonight. He knew it, and so did the contenders in the other cells. All glowing eyes, all hungry, all looking at the ripped-up werewolf who couldn't even hide his limp anymore. Fuck, Roman hoped he didn't draw Hays. His inner wolf was already on the verge of the same insanity that the others were fighting just from the kills he'd done. He didn't want to do this. Didn't want to be here.

The hanging lightbulb above Roman's cell flickered, casting everything in eerie shadows. He was growing hungry for something he didn't understand. Blood maybe. He'd had moments of dread for the next fight, but over the last few hours, as they'd pulled wolf after wolf, he'd begun feeling something different. Something that unsettled him. Bloodlust.

The wolves at the end had been here the longest. Roman bit the tape and began wrapping his other hand as he watched the big brawlers in the last two cells. They were both watching Hays with snarled lips, as though they wanted to eat him while they were still human. Two psychopaths, who had probably been decent guys before Anderson bought them. Now they were empty shells with nothing but darkness inside of them. Killing unnecessarily did that to werewolves. It ruined them. Already, Roman could feel it ruining him, too.

Dad stood in the corner of his cell. At least he wasn't going to die alone, so there was that. God, he couldn't think like that. He had to get out of this somehow, get back to Mila, let her heal his damaged soul. He would never tell her about what had happened here, but he could find sanctuary in her embrace.

The door on the opposite wall swung open, and a behemoth strode in, eyes glowing gold. Anderson. Fucking traitor werewolf, pitting his own kind against each other for money. Roman was going to kill him. He didn't know how yet, but if it was the last thing he did, he would end that asshole for all he'd taken from this world. He would bet his jeep Rhett had sold some of his pack to Anderson when they'd defied him. Anderson kept hinting that Rhett always gave him the best fighters. None of the wolves in here were familiar, so the other Bone-Rippers were probably long dead.

He tracked Anderson's progress down the line of cells. He held a cattle prod, the contraption sparking electricity at the end like it was ready to zap the shit out of one of them. Again. Roman had been on the end of that thing a dozen times already. Roman snarled when Anderson locked eyes with him as he passed and smiled. He'd filed his teeth to sharp points and looked half Changed already. He lived for pain.

"Hays, you're up."

Shit. "Against who?" Roman asked, ripping the tape and testing the tightness of the wrap on his knuckles.

"Don't worry, Striker, you'll get your shot to bleed someone tonight. Your eyes say you're ready. I haven't seen human color in them for twenty-four hours. I think you're ready for a brawl with one of the beasts," Anderson said, gesturing to the psychopaths on the end. "Hays isn't for you. You'd kill him in fifteen seconds flat, and what fun would that be for a crowd? None. He's food for Brayah tonight."

Roman's heart sank to his feet. Brayah, female, middle of a pack dominance but a fighter. She was brought in the same day as Roman. She must've won her last match. Two matches back-to-back could be her end, even if it was with an injured wolf. "You just fought her."

"When I want your opinion on matches, I'll ask. The customers like the girl. They like when she wins. They want the double match, and they get what they want," he said, rubbing his fingers together in a money gesture. "Sit tight, Striker. You're next. Grand finale tonight, you lucky dog, you. So many requests for the rogue. You've got fans out there." Anderson charged the cell but stopped right as he reached the bars. With an evil grin, he murmured, "I've got something special in store for you. Enjoy your last breaths."

When Anderson walked to Hays's cell and opened the creaking metal door, the wolf didn't even fight it. His eyes had dimmed, and he carried his head and tail low as though he'd already accepted defeat. Hays ghosted him a glance as he trotted by. Roman wished he could say something encouraging to light a fire under him, but then he'd be telling him to kill Brayah.

Everything in this hell was so messed up.

Enjoy your last breaths.

Roman dragged his gaze to the brawlers at the end, then closed his eyes and imagined Mila's face. Good, light, smiling. She was the happy place he disappeared to when the dark thoughts filled his head. When he had moments of weakness and wanted to give up, her face was what he imagined to get him fighting again. He couldn't turn into Hays. He had to keep winning until he could figure out a way to escape this place.

She wasn't safe until Rhett was cold and in the ground, and Roman's brothers couldn't protect her until they understood the danger. Rhett was a silver bullet in the heart of the werewolves of Rangeley, and that monster had his sights on Mila.

One way or another, Roman had to get back to her.

SIXTEEN

"You look fine," Blaire whispered, grasping Mila's hand.

Mila stopped fiddling with the rips in her skin-tight, black skinny jeans and held Blaire's hand like a scared child. Terror had crept inside her and made a home in her chest, and she needed to steady out, fast.

Up front, Asher was quiet as the night, eyes drifting occasionally to his phone where he was tracking Rhett. Gentry was sitting in the front seat, staring out the window. He would snarl low, stop himself, and then start back up a few seconds later.

"Cut that shit out. You'll set me off," Asher growled. When he looked over at Gentry, his eyes were nearly white.

Mila whined, but swallowed hard and forced herself to stop. "Gentry, seriously don't set him off in here." She rolled down the window and sucked the freezing cold air in hopes to relieve the heaviness that had settled over her.

Now leaving Rangeley. Mila stared in shock as they passed the sign. That used to be one of the boundaries. How many hours had she spent testing the line, trying to escape this place, and suddenly, she was past it, blasting down the road in a truck full of dominant werewolves. Her life sure had taken a strange turn. Strange. Ha. Maybe Rangeley should be called Strangeley.

Blaire was wearing a short leather skirt over fishnet stockings and black combat boots. Her sweater had diamond shapes cut out of the sides, and her red hair was curled and flowing down her shoulders. She'd done dark make-up around her eyes, making them look even brighter green. She smelled scared, too, but her hand clutched in Mila's was steady.

Mila blew out a long breath and glanced up in the rearview mirror. Blaire had done her make-up and trimmed her bangs. Her eyeshadow was shimmery black, and Blaire had done thick eye-liner that made her look like she had cat-eyes. Her dark hair was curled in thick waves and trailing down her shoulders. Her black sweater was all ripped up, showing her sides, her arms, her collar bones, her cleavage. God, she looked so different from what she was used to. It was a total transformation. At least she was wearing boots with thick heels. Easier for running and/or kicking peoples' teeth in, she supposed.

The next hour felt like hell. The evening shadows morphed to full dark, and it started snowing again. The churning clouds above blotted out the moon and stars, and even with her heightened vision, the woods that passed outside the window looked too dark, too haunted.

Roman. She couldn't even imagine what was happening to him, and waves of panic overtook her every few minutes with an urgency to get to him. To make sure he was okay.

"You would feel it if he were dead," Asher said in a voice too gravelly to be human.

Chills rippled up her arms. "What do you mean?"

Asher turned onto a worn dirt path off the main.

"He's not dead. You're bound. You would be dead, too."

"Stop fucking doing that, man!" Gentry barked. "I don't even want to know what you did to yourself to be able to guess people's thoughts, but stay out of our heads."

"Bound?"

"I can see it," Asher said in that demon voice of his. "It's purple. Dark. It's always moving, like fog, but when you and Roman are together, it stays between you, connecting you. I saw it when you were kids, too, but it was faint. Roman fought it. Gentry and Blaire have one too, but theirs is blue."

"Like fog," Blaire said in a strange tone as she stared at the back of Asher's dirty blond hair. "I saw that when Odine was saving me. There was blue fog that kept reaching for Gentry. Every time I opened my eyes, it was there between us. Asher, are you like Odine?"

"We're here," he ground out.

Sure enough there were rows of cars and trucks in an old, cracked parking lot, but there was no building. There were just transmission towers and a bunch of complicated-looking electrical equipment built on a gravel lot, surrounded by barbed wire fencing.

Asher and Gentry didn't seem deterred, though. They both wore black sweaters and black pants over dark boots. Without a word, they each pulled a black winter hat low over their foreheads and shoved their doors open like they'd trained for this. It was good, though. They seemed confident, so it bolstered Mila's bravery a little.

"I'll be with you," Blaire said low. "We'll have each other's backs, okay? Let's go get your mate back."

"My mate," Mila whispered as Blaire got out of the truck. She didn't wear a jacket so Mila left hers on the seat and slid out of the jacked-up truck behind Blaire. Asher was already striding for the trees, as if he knew exactly where he was going, so they followed, Mila jogging to catch up.

Blaire cast her a glance over her shoulder. "Mila, chin up my strong girl. Shoulders back, don't let them see your weak side. Don't let that gaze drop to the ground. Not tonight. If anyone asks questions, speak like you know what you're talking about."

"Big bad wolf tonight," Mila said on a shaky breath.

"Hell, yeah," Blaire murmured with a nod. Her eyes were glowing brighter green now. Mila's were probably the color of champagne, but it couldn't be helped.

Thanks to the high-heeled boots, it felt like they hiked two miles into the dark woods, but it was probably no more than two hundred yards. There were four men standing like sentries, two on either side of a door of an impossibly small building. Their eyes were glowing as they checked the ID of a man at the front of a line five-men deep. One of them glanced up when Asher led them to the end of the line. He nodded a suspicious greeting and went back to checking a list pinned to a clipboard.

One spoke into a radio about the man who had been approved and coming down stairs. Okay, so the small building was probably just a stairwell that led underground.

Mila got more nervous when they opened the door and allowed the man into the dark building, then shut the door again. By the time there were only two men left in the line in front of them, Mila's heart was hammering, and her breath was coming in shallow pants.

Asher looked over his shoulder at her, snarled up his lip, and bore his white teeth in the dark. "Settle," he demanded as soft as a breath.

Her inner wolf sank down deep inside of her, and Mila had to grit her teeth against the whine that clawed its way up her throat. Asher kept staring at her with those blazing silver eyes, and whatever he was doing was working because Mila could finally drag in a long breath. A steadying one.

The wolves on duty were huge. Massive chests, powerful arms, thick necks, at least six-five, all of them. They smelled like dominant titans. They looked like Asher and Gentry. Problem number one: there were four of them but only two of the Striker brothers.

Problem two: a trio of human men appeared on the trail through the woods, talking low about some, "Finale fight," and in front of Mila, Asher and Gentry looked at each other. She didn't know what they said to each other with those looks, but they both nodded at the same time.

Blaire hooked her finger under Mila's chin and lifted it. In the dim light, she arched her eyebrow in a gentle reminder to watch her posture. Oh, yeah.

Mila inhaled deeply and straightened her spine as the last guy in line was allowed through the door. They were up now, and surrounded, because the guys from the woods were now standing in line behind them. Mila's inner wolf writhed to Change and flee. Fuck.

She closed her eyes and blew out a soft breath as Asher stepped up to the guy with the list. Surely he had a plan, or a name to give them, but nope, Asher just reached forward in one blurred, graceful motion and snapped the man's neck. The break sounded like gunfire in the woods. Mila stood there frozen as Gentry slammed his fist into another guard's face.

The line behind them surged forward, yelling. One started running off, but Blaire tripped him and dragged him back, shoved him toward where Gentry and Asher were engaged in a violence Mila couldn't take her frozen gaze away from.

Mila.

She got shoved hard in the back.

Mila.

She slammed into the side of the building.

"Mila!" Gentry said, yanking her toward the door.

Blaire was already standing in the open frame,

gesturing for her to hurry. The oldest Striker brother was at war with two of the guards. And Asher, Mila realized, was really, truly good at war.

Stunned, she bolted for Blaire and slipped into the darkness with her. She skidded down two stairs and caught herself on the railing as something slammed against the door behind them. *Please don't let that be one of our guys.*

Blaire gave her a bright-eyed look and whispered, "Let's go."

A wave of protectiveness washed through Mila. Blaire looked scared, too, and it changed something inside of her. She would have Blaire's back tonight, no matter what.

Steeling herself, Mila whispered, "It's me and you. Okay?"

Blaire nodded once, but the whites of her eyes were showing around her irises. She was a new werewolf, new to the violence of this life. Mila took her hand and led her carefully down the dim stairwell.

At the bottom was a long hallway lit by hanging lightbulbs. The walls on either side were painted in murals with horrifying scenes of beasts ripping into each other. The place smelled like blood and made her wolf draw up inside of her—not to run, but to be wary.

There was a man at the end, guarding a heavy-looking metal door. He smelled human, thank God. Humans were easy to lie to. Still, he was huge, dressed in all black, and was twirling a giant knife in his hands. He glared them down as he held up the radio to his lips. "Sanger, what's going on? Are these girls good?"

He took his thumb off the button and waited as static blasted across the radio.

"Is there a problem?" Blaire asked, calm-as-you-like. She was looking him dead in the eyes like a badass. Okay then.

Mila glared at him, too, and canted her head. Hopefully the lights were dim enough to hide her eye-color.

"Sanger," the guy asked again. "Let them pass or no?"

"Seriously?" Mila asked Blaire. "We drove all the way out here for this shit?"

Blaire shook her head like she was pissed. "Maybe we should take our money elsewhere. I wanted to see the finale, but this feels sketchy." She turned to leave and Mila made to follow.

"Wait!" the guard barked. "Sanger," he barked into the radio.

"They're fine," came the answer.

Sure sounded like Asher's voice, but the guard yelled into the radio, "Dammit, Anderson told you to answer immediately. If you have to take a shit, hold it until after the fight." The guard jammed his radio in the sling at his hip and twirled the knife again like he was showing off. He dragged his eyes down Mila's body and gave a wolfish grin. "You like bloodbaths then."

Mila's stomach curdled, but she answered, "I don't trust people who don't enjoy a good bloodbath."

The guy licked his bottom lip and nodded like *hell yeah*, then gave three knocks on the metal door and yanked it open. "Enjoy the show, ladies. Come see me after if it revs you up." As Mila followed Blaire through, he murmured too close to Mila's ear, "I'll take good care of you." Lie. His voice held a big lie. *Monster*.

She forced herself not to shrink away from him and gave him a wicked smile instead. "Aw, don't tease me now. I may take you up on that." When she turned around, she gave a terrified look to the back of Blaire's head and tried her best to sashay her hips as she made her way down a short hallway that opened up to a bigger room.

The sound of cheering, stomping, clapping, and whistling was deafening, and for a moment, Mila stood next to Blaire in stunned awe. The place was huge. She couldn't have imagined a place like this could exist out here. It was well lit, so she could see everything clearly. In the center of the room was a huge dome-shaped metal cage. Around it were tons of people crowded, cheering. On the walls, there were fancy box seats, like they were in an old-fashioned theater. Men in suits sipping drinks sat there looking down at the cage.

Down on the lower level, Blaire and Mila were dressed just right. There weren't many girls, but the ones here were wearing the same kind of get-up. Along one wall were mattresses with transparent curtains. On the beds, where everyone could see, couples were openly having sex.

"Oh, my gosh," Mila said on a breath. There was something in the air here, something awful, a destructive energy that pressed against her shoulders.

"Come on," Blaire said, ripping her gaze away from some guy giving it doggy style to a girl wearing white make-up and nothing but a black leather corset. "We need to find Roman and get out of here."

"Drinks?" a girl dressed in a see-through net bodysuit asked. Her eyes were hazy and her make-up smeared, but she held a tray of blue shots steady enough.

"Sure," Mila said, taking one. Go with the flow and all, but the second the nearly-naked server walked off, she and Blaire looked at each other and subtly sniffed the drinks. They smelled drugged. Nope. They both emptied them out nonchalantly on the dirt floor as they made their way toward the cage.

Mila had a really bad feeling about what they would find there. A huge part of her didn't want to look, but she knew she had to. Blaire grabbed her hand when she slowed and pulled her through the crowd. It was so tight around the cage, and the men were groping Mila and Blaire both as they moved farther in, but they didn't quit until they were on the rail, within arm's length of the wide bars.

"I wouldn't touch that," a tall, lanky man beside Mila advised. He tossed his empty drink cup at it, and sparks flew. Mila stared in horror as the half melted plastic cup hit the ground. "They electrify it to keep the wolves from escaping and biting us. Pretty clever, huh?"

Right now, there was nothing in the enormous cage. "Is it over?" she asked, daring to lock eyes on his.

Excitement flashed across his face. "That one is. Too quick if you ask me, but Anderson's set up another double feature."

Mila forced a smile and hoped it looked excited and not disgusted. "What's that? It's my first time here?"

"Are you fucking serious?" the guy asked, grinning so big. He would've been handsome if not for the stink of absolute darkness on him. "God, I can't wait to watch your face. First fights...there's nothing like them," he said dreamily. He maneuvered himself behind her and locked his arms on either side of the rail around her, trapping her. "I'm Shane."

"She's mine," Blaire said.

"Your girlfriend?"

"I like to call her my mate," Blaire said with a flirty smile.

The man didn't back off an inch. "Role-playing, I like that. And you both wear the bright contacts. I'm thinking of having my teeth filed."

"Mmm," Mila said. "So sexy." *Barf.* "So explain the double feature."

"Oh, you'll love it. Anderson—he runs this place—well, he got his hands on some super-bloodline of werewolf a couple days ago. That's why the crowd's so fucking *big* right now. He's a total brawler. I saw him fight last night. A ripper, dead eyes, massive wolf. Born to be a slayer, he has the genetics to be a legend here. Anderson's gonna give him to one of his pets first, see if he can pull out a win and prove himself."

A man appeared from the side door of the cage, and Blaire lurched forward, dropping her plastic shot glass against the bar like it was an accident. No sparks. Mila and Blaire locked gazes, and Blaire jerked her chin toward the door. Mila got it. There had to be a switch over there that turned off the electric current when someone was entering or exiting the arena.

"I'm gonna go to the bathroom," Blaire said, shoving off the railing.

"Now?" Shane asked, his eyebrows arched high.

Blaire gave an empty smile as she passed. "I'm meeting someone in there."

"Oh, shit. Get it, girl," Shane said with a perverted chuckle.

Mila didn't like being split up from Blaire at all. And it wasn't just because she was alone with Shane, who still had her trapped against the railing. It was because she couldn't protect Blaire if they weren't together.

The bruiser who had entered the ring lifted his hands, and the cheers became so loud Mila hunched at the pain in her ears. He played it up for a while, putting on a show, and then finally he tamped his hands down and settled the crowd.

"That's Anderson," Shane whispered in her ear. Mila wanted to punch him in the throat, but forced herself to stay still.

"Ladies and gentle-monsters, do I have a treat for you tonight!" He gestured to the door, and two men strode in, graceful, muscled-up, scarred, bruised, cut, battered, dirty. The first one she didn't recognize at all, but the second she knew from scent alone, even before she could see him from behind the other titan.

"Roman," she murmured.

His eyes had been on the ground, but at her soft whisper, he lifted his gaze directly to her. A moment of recognition sparked there, but then he tore his gaze from her quickly. She'd seen it, though. The haunted emptiness in his eyes that hadn't been there before.

Anderson had been talking, revving up the crowd, but Mila's head was filled with only a roaring sound as Roman made his way to one side of the cage and walked the edge slowly, glaring at the crowd as Anderson introduced him. He stopped before he got to Mila, then paced the other way, every rigid muscle tense as he clenched his wrapped fists. Why wouldn't he look at her? She was right here. Why wouldn't he look?

Closing the gap on seven feet tall and heavily muscled, the other guy was massive with a black mohawk. Tattoos covered his upper torso, arms, and neck. His eyes were what scared her the most. Such a light brown, and completely empty. Just...dead as he watched Roman pacing across the arena. He probably had been handsome once before he turned killer. Anderson introduced him as Slade.

Anderson left the arena, and Roman scanned the curve of the cage above him. He was breathing faster now. God, he looked like a warrior, all streaked with blood and grit and dirt, his six-pack flexing with every breath, his shoulders bulging, his eyes the color of melted gold.

Look at me!

"If he wins this match, he'll fight again immediately," Shane explained too close to her ear.

"Back off her," Roman snarled, jamming a finger immediately at Shane.

"Whoa," Shane said, easing off her by inches.

Roman's face was twisted up in a feral look that dumped terror into her middle. She almost didn't recognize him. It was as if his smile lines didn't exist anymore. He twitched his attention to the brawler approaching him slowly. "Mila, get out of here," he murmured so low she could barely make it out over the cheering of the crowd.

He had to live. She couldn't just leave right now while he was about to do this. Two fights would determine whether he would keep breathing, and either way, she had to stand behind him. Had to figure out a way to help. "Who does he fight next?"

Shane pointed across the arena. "Him."

Rhett stood there against the railing, his chin lifted high as he stared down at Mila with a satisfied expression. He didn't look weak anymore, and his neck was healing quickly now. Perhaps Odine's magic didn't reach this far. His eyes matched the brawler stalking Roman—dead.

Of course he would make sure Roman was exhausted from a battle before he challenged him. Rhett had no honor.

Coward, she mouthed as fury pounded through her veins.

A slow, evil smile stretched his lips as though the insult meant nothing to him. *I win, Bottom Bitch.*

She hated him. This was all his doing. His fault. He was supplying wolves to this place. This was where half of the Bone-Rippers had disappeared to. He'd brought the ones who defied him here, to this hellhole. And then he'd fought them against other supes like they were nothing. Like they didn't matter, but they did. They had. They mattered to her.

A long, low snarl rattled through her before she

could stop it. Shane backed off like a clever little human who'd just figured out he was standing too close to death. She wanted to bite him just for watching this shit. Just for being here. Werewolves weren't the animals here. It was these people, screaming for blood, their eyes bright with excitement at the thought of senseless death. Bloodthirsty monsters. Now she understood why Odine had been scared for Roman. Mila spun a slow circle and looked around at the cheering, jeering crowd, crying out for blood. For Roman's blood. Might as well be her blood.

Behind her, she heard and felt Roman clash with the titan. When she turned around, Roman had him up in the air. He slammed him to the ground, then went to town pummeling his face. Three hits, and Slade bucked him off and swung his fist at Roman's face. He rolled at the last second, and Slade bellowed as his hand crashed onto the dirt floor with a crack. Dirt exploded where he connected. The fight lasted for an eternity, or for a few seconds, it didn't matter. Every moment was agony on Mila's wolf as she stood there helpless, watching the man she loved fight for his life. They locked up so many times, traded punches, traded cracked ribs and split lips. Traded their souls to the darkness maybe because the longer the fight went on, the deader Roman's eyes looked. Senseless war was ruining his wolf. Mila didn't want to watch, but couldn't take her eyes away from Roman's lethal grace. They went to blows, hitting, locking up, hitting, locking up, until in a rush, Roman threw Slade against the cage.

"Oh, my gosh," Mila said, wincing away as the metal hummed the second Slade connected with it. His body went rigid right before he slammed to the ground.

Relief welled inside of her as Roman stalked the titan.

"Change!" Shane yelled. And it wasn't just him. Others in the crowd were yelling the same thing.

"Change, Change, Change." It became a chant, and Roman froze, looking down at Slade, his face completely void of any emotion. He looked like a robot, and a wave of nausea took Mila's stomach.

"Change," Anderson yelled from where he stood by Rhett across the arena.

Roman went to his hands and knees, fists clenched before he let the wolf rip from his skin.

It was taking Blaire too long to cut the power to the cage. Something was wrong, and when Mila scanned frantically the masses, Blaire was nowhere to be seen. Fuck waiting around, she had to move now. She bolted through the crowd, pushing and elbowing to make room. There was this humming sensation pressing against her chest that she didn't understand. It smelled faintly familiar in here, too. It was like Odine's magic, but different. Darker.

Something bad was happening. Something so bad. Where the fuck was Blaire? The snarling of the wolves filled her head, and her animal pushed to Change. It wouldn't do any good, though. It would just expose her before she could get to Roman.

"Owooooooooooooooo," she howled, head snapping back toward the ceiling, calling…something. Crying for something she didn't understand. Begging help.

The crowd around her froze for one single moment, and then panic ensued, as they tried to get away from her.

"She's one of them!"

"One of the wolves got loose!"

She snarled at a man who reached for her, sank

her teeth into his hand. *Don't fucking touch me.* "Owoooooooo!"

The crowd parted as she jumped up onto the railing that surrounded the cage. Roman and Slade were ripping each other to shreds. The scent of heavy magic thickened the air and clogged her throat, and when she looked back at the panicking crowd, she saw them. Gentry was in wolf form engaged with another werewolf she didn't recognize. One of the guards perhaps. It was Asher who held her attention, though. He was in human form, but his eyes were white and roiling with fury as he strode toward her. His muscular neck arched back as he answered her call. "Owooooo!" His voice sounded haunted. The note died in his throat as he threw up a hand toward the ceiling in a quick gesture that had an immediate reaction. Every light above them exploded, raining sparks.

Asher gave her a bone-chilling smile as the shadows took him, as if he was most comfortable in darkness.

"No!" Rhett screamed above the frantic crowd, who were filtering out of the exit in droves.

"Done!" Blaire yelled from somewhere to the left.

The humming died from the cage. "Mila, get him out of there!"

Thank God. Mila turned, grabbed the metal, and braced herself against the railing. Pushing her body, she pried the bars as hard as she could. And then she wasn't alone. Gentry was still at war behind them, but Asher jumped up on the railing and took the bars in his hands, then ripped it apart like it was paper. Mila had only moved it a couple inches, but Asher had torn a mother-fucking hole in the cage.

There was light filtering in through the open exit door, and she could now see Roman and Slade killing each other. Asher was ripped backward off the railing by three bright-eyed guards, but Mila was already too far out of their reach, no help to Asher right now. Not when her focus was on saving Roman.

She slipped through the hole in the bars and cried out with the pain of the Change. It came so fast, as if her wolf had been waiting for her feet to touch the ground to steal her body. Something massive whooshed past her, and she snarled as another big wolf attacked Roman. She'd bet her bones it was Anderson. Now it was two on one and Roman needed help, now.

So she—submissive little chicken—bolted for the wolf fight, sank her teeth into Anderson's neck, and shook her head as hard as she could to do the most damage.

He released Roman's shoulder with a snarl, but Slade and Roman were still locked onto each other's necks.

"Mila!" Asher yelled. "Don't let him take alpha!"

What? That made no sense. The distraction almost made her lose her death grip on the massive wolf.

Something barreled into her and knocked her against the rails. With a snarl, Mila righted herself and glared at her assailant. Dread pulsed through her body when she saw the giant gray wolf. *Alpha. No.* She shook her head, trying to rattle her wolf off her urge to cower in front of Rhett.

Anderson was laying limp on the ground, and Slade was on the run, bolting for the opening in the cage, but Rhett was circling Roman now. And God, Roman looked like he'd already been through hell. His gray fur was matted and wet with crimson, but he didn't favor any injuries. His head was lowered, his red teeth bared, his hackles raised all down his back.

His eyes blazed like fire. Beautiful destroyer.

Behind him, Blaire's winter-white wolf appeared like an apparition, her lips curled back over razor sharp teeth.

My pack. Mila slunk around the cage and forced herself to Roman. She cowered under Rhett's glare, but placed herself under Roman's chin to protect his throat. Slowly, eyes locked on Rhett's, she pulled her lips back from her teeth and growled. *Mine.*

Move. She could hear him so clearly in her mind, but she forced her body to stay still. Roman was warm and alive against her back, and if she had to bring hell to earth, she was going to keep it that way.

Rhett paced, his ears erect, his eyes filled with hate. He snarled a terrifying sound. *Move!*

Mila jerked her head but didn't move. She'd thought this whole time she would never rid herself of Rhett's poisonous alpha bond unless she found another alpha, or unless Odine had mercy on her and ripped the bond from her soul with magic. But in this moment, Mila felt the change. The urge to obey died to nothing. She didn't choose him as her alpha anymore, so he had no power over her.

Roman had lifted her up too high, and now she

was nobody's Bottom Bitch.

The snarl in her throat rattled louder. *Fffuck you.*

She could tell the instant Rhett decided she was expendable. The moment he knew he'd lost her for always. The moment he decided he would rather kill her than share her with Roman. It was in his furious icy blue eyes. Murder dwelled there.

He went for her face, but Roman was on him, tearing into his ear, ripping him backward as Rhett's teeth snapped an inch away from Mila's muzzle. And Roman wasn't alone. Blaire engaged, and so did Mila. The snarling was deafening, but Mila was completely calm as she fought. The pain felt like nothing, and nothing around her mattered except for Roman and Blaire. If they were okay, she was okay. More than okay. She was the bone-ripper. She would burn the world to the fucking ground if it meant the ones she loved were safe.

Blaire was thrown off and, worried over her friend, Mila lost her grip. Roman was shredding Rhett's throat. It wouldn't be long now.

Time slowed to a crawl.

Blaire lay on her side near the bars, struggling to her feet.

Asher's tar-black wolf looked panicked as he ran toward them through the hole in the cage, silver eyes on Roman.

Gentry ran behind him, eyes wide with warning. They were charging in to stop Roman.

Don't let him take alpha.

Roman wasn't meant for that role, had never wanted it, but he was killing the alpha of the Bone-Rippers. That fucked-up pack would be his under technicality. And already his soul was on the edge of darkness. The last two days had deadened his eyes, and Mila could see them—his ghosts stood around the edge of the cage, gathering by the dozens, staring at him with such sadness in their eyes. Noah was here, and he locked eyes with her. He shook his head. *Not him*, he mouthed.

This wasn't how it was supposed to be. Roman already shouldered too much.

Asher and Gentry wouldn't make it in time, neither would Blaire, but Mila could fix this for him.

She slammed into Roman, knocking him off Rhett, and then Mila—little chicken Mila—latched her teeth onto Rhett's throat and finished him.

SEVENTEEN

Alpha. Mila tested out the word in her mind, but it meant nothing right now. She waited for the adrenaline dump to make her shake like a leaf, but it didn't come as she stood there numb, newly Changed back to her human form, watching Roman stand slowly. He was covered in bruises, bites, scratches, new scars. His lip was split, and blood trickled from his ear down the tattoos on his neck. He wouldn't meet her gaze, but he made his way out of the cage and picked up something from the ground. It was a discarded jacket from one of the monsters. He strode back in and settled it gently over her shoulders, as if trying not to touch her. As if trying not to taint her.

Mila's heart ached for him.

"Stay here," he murmured in a voice that couldn't pass for human. "I'm releasing the others. Don't let them near you."

"I'll come with you," Mila murmured. "I can help."

"No," Roman said too fast. "I don't want you to see."

And the ache in her heart deepened.

He was protecting her, but he had to hide what he'd been through to do it. She wanted all of him, but now he wouldn't be able to give that to her.

Asher, Gentry, and Blaire had disappeared into a back room as soon as they Changed back, so Mila stood alone, watching the man she loved walk out of the cage door and back into the hell he'd been through over the last couple of days.

There were five men and one woman who came out of the door a few minutes later. None of them looked okay, and they all smelled sick. Not body sick. Soul sick. Mila pressed her back against the cage as the biggest one locked his dead eyes on her as he strode by. She wasn't scared, though. Not like she used to be. Something was different inside of her now. She'd broken in a strange way and didn't want to cower to people anymore. Or maybe she was just exhausted. Maybe her submissiveness would come back in the morning.

Roman was wearing a pair of jeans when he came back, ripped up at the knees. Maybe they were his. They fit him well. He was cleaning dirt off his chest with a T-shirt that he tossed onto Rhett's still wolf as he passed. "Let's go," he gritted out.

"What about Asher and the others?"

"They're going to burn this place to the ground." Along with Rhett. But he didn't have to say that part. It was implied.

Roman's back was tense as he made his way toward the exit. She didn't understand. Mila was desperate to touch him, to reassure herself that he was okay. That he was alive and breathing and warm and still hers. But Roman didn't seem to want touch. He didn't seem to want any attention at all.

He looked massive, shoulders bulging, veins popping, dirt smeared on his body, tattoos stark against his pale skin. Mila followed him out of the exit and up the stairs. He took them two at a time like he was trying to get away from her, but she wouldn't let him. So she stalked him steadily, matched his pace, was nice and quiet. She followed him of the door at the top of the stairs and into the frosty night air. She followed him down the worn path in the woods, then trailed him still when he veered off into the trees. She came to a stop when he approached an old, gnarly pine tree and slammed his closed fists against it. Body rigid, he rested his forehead onto the trunk, his back to Mila.

"You shouldn't see me like this." It was like when they were kids in the woods all over again, the night before he left. Well, she would be damned if he left her now.

"Yes, I should, Roman. Good side or bad side, you're mine. Shadows and all." She approached slowly and ran her palm slowly up the rigid muscles of his back. "I'm not going anywhere."

His voice came out hoarse when he said, "Blaire told me the first time she met Odine, the witch said I was on the fence. One side is good and one side is evil, and she didn't know which way I would jump. Mila, I…" He covered his face with his hands and yelled long and loud, his body convulsing with the sound.

Tears filled Mila's eyes and streamed down her cheeks as she slid her arms around his middle and rested her face against his spine. "Shhhhh. Roman, you have one foot on that dark side, I understand. But baby, you always have. Those shadows are a part of your make-up. A part of you. No one can manage them like you. No one, you understand? You stay on that fence, Roman. That's your burden, and when the dark gets too tempting, look to your right. Close your eyes, Roman. Can you see me? I'm standing here, white dress, wild grass up to my hips, hair lifting in the wind, blue sky, sunshine, and I'm smiling up at you because I *know* you've got this. When the shadows get tempting, keep your eyes on me. I don't mind sharing you with the dark, but always come back to me."

Roman spun in her arms and pulled her against his chest as his lips crashed onto hers. His teeth grazed her lips, and his tongue plunged into her mouth hard, over and over. His grip was rough in her hair, but she didn't mind. She would take him rough right now if it meant he was still here with her. And he needed this. It was so clear he needed her to make the ghosts go away for a little while. So she reached for the snap of his jeans and unfastened them, shoved them halfway down his hips as he walked her backward.

With a snarl, he lifted her up to straddle his hips, and she held onto him tight, encasing them both in the oversize jacket she wore. Teeth, teeth, teeth. Roman was going to be bitey tonight, but she didn't care. It turned her on. Relief flowed through her as he let her back in, kiss by kiss. He was letting her hold his broken soul in her hands for safekeeping until he was strong enough to bear the pain of it again.

"I love you," she whispered, because he should hear her devotion. She was still in this, still with him, no matter what.

The snarl in his throat grew louder as he gripped her body tighter and ground his hips against hers. Felt so good when he hit her clit just right. Mila locked her legs around him and threw her head back as he grazed his teeth against her throat.

Roman eased her to the ground, but that was as far as his gentleness went tonight. He sank his teeth into her shoulder as he pushed into her hard, then released her torn skin with a groan. There was no urge to cower, or obey. There was no alpha bond. Mila was her own alpha now, and Roman could keep his freedom. They worked best like this, separate but together. He reared back and slid into her again and again, hard, desperate. She understood. She needed the exact same right now.

Mila cried out at the heat he created in her center. That erotic tingling sensation he could conjure so easily in her. His abs flexed with every hard stroke inside her. His body was like a stone when she ran her nails down the curves of his shoulders. His arm wrapped under her lower back, and then he bucked into her faster. So...fucking...perfect.

Mila arched her back against the ground and looked up at the full moon sitting low in the sky. So close. Pressure built every time his thick shaft slid into her. Orgasm exploded through her just as he pushed in deep and poured warmth into her. He smoothed out his rhythm and drew out her aftershocks as he spilled his seed, filling her, warming her from the inside out.

When their aftershocks slowed, and then faded completely, he rolled to the side and dragged her body against his. He buried his face in her neck and inhaled deeply, over and over, as though her scent steadied him. Mila ran her nails lightly up and down his back until the tension in his muscles began to soften.

"I see you," he whispered. "White dress, smiling up at me. I see you."

Mila nuzzled her face against his neck as a warm tear slipped out of the corner of her eye. "I see you, too."

EIGHTEEN

One week, and Winter's Edge would be open again, not only to werewolves, but to the humans of this town, too. It would be like old days, but different. Mila smiled absently as she dried a glass. She'd poured her heart into this place over the last few weeks with the Strikers and Blaire because she wanted what they wanted. She wanted Noah's legacy to live on. She wanted this town to eventually get back to the way it was. She wanted this place to feel like home again.

Roman slipped his hands around her waist and pressed against her back as he kissed her neck. He'd been hauling in supplies with Gentry and Asher all morning while she and Blaire readied the bar area for the grand opening.

He inhaled deeply, right at her hair line, and murmured, "I'm glad you don't wear your hair in your face anymore. I like being able to see your eyes."

Mila giggled and leaned into him. He liked her strong, and there was something so empowering about that.

"Have you made a decision yet?"

Mila turned in his arms and slid her hands up around his neck, hugged him tight. He was asking her if she was ready to take the throne of the Bone-Rippers, but she'd been putting it off. She was alpha by technicality, but she'd also watched the pack stand by and let awful things happen under Rhett. And while the investigation about his disappearance was happening, she just didn't feel a rush to bind the wolves of Rangeley to her.

"I'm not ready today, but I will be. I'm close."

Roman pressed his lips gently to hers. When he eased back by inches, he cupped her cheeks, and his eyes held hers. They were blue for the first time since the wolf fights, and such a tidal wave of relief washed over her.

"Alpha Mila. That's so fucking hot." He dragged

her hand to his crotch where he was rocking one giant boner.

She laughed and shook her head, her cheeks heating with happiness.

"Ugh, stop," Asher drawled unhappily from where he carried a box out of the kitchen. "I'm so fucking tired of watching your disgusting—"

"Sexy and necessary," Roman corrected.

"—perverted displays of affection," Asher gritted out like Roman hadn't interrupted at all. "Are you ready to do this or what?"

"Do what?" Mila asked with a frown.

"You'll see," Roman said, his eyes sparking with excitement.

"Go on a hike to the peak," Asher muttered.

"Dude, it was a surprise."

Asher settled the box on a table and tossed Roman a remorseless look. "And we're taking pictures." Asher flipped Roman off and disappeared into the kitchen.

"He's not excited," Roman said through a grin.

"Is that why you're making him do it?"

Roman looked downright naughty when he murmured, "Maybe. What's that mushy look for?"

Mila stroked her hands down his beard. "There was this moment, right after the fights, when you wouldn't let me touch you, when I thought I lost you. And then I stayed scared because you weren't joking, playing, or laughing for weeks." Mila lowered her voice to a whisper. "But today you feel like my Roman again."

He let off a soft, sexy growl and nipped at her neck. "I feel more like myself today, too. You wanna go make out in the freezer?"

Mila opened her mouth to say "yes," but Asher answered for her from the kitchen. "No! We're all waiting on you. Hurry up!"

Roman waggled his eyebrows and said, "Raincheck," then dragged her by the hand through the kitchen and out the back door.

She only had on a sweater, leggings, and snow boots, but there were no humans around and no reason to pretend she got cold. Plus, Blaire was currently climbing on Gentry like a backpack, clad in only a thin long-sleeved shirt and bootcut jeans, so okay. The peak wasn't that long of a hike anyway.

Asher led the way, so far ahead she lost sight of him a few times, but Gentry and Blaire stayed close, chattering happily with Mila and Roman. Twice, Roman turned to help her up steep rocks. He'd kiss her knuckles when she was safely to him, then would continue talking as though he didn't even realize he was giving the affection. Oh, this man. He owned her heart without even trying. And it wasn't scary like she'd thought love like this would be. She'd given her heart willingly because she trusted him.

The snow was fresh and crunched under their boots. Mila and Blaire's laughter echoed through the hills, and everything was perfect. As they made it to the top of the incline, huffing and puffing frozen breath, Mila was struck with how beautiful this moment was. The sun was setting in a half-circle right at the edge of the horizon, casting the valley in gold light and deep shadows, making the new snow sparkle like God had dumped glitter on the landscape.

Asher was setting up a tripod and camera, right along the tree line, facing the cliff edge they used to sit on as kids.

Mila slowed and tugged at Roman's hand. "What's going on?" she asked.

He squared up to her, pulled a folded photograph from his back pocket, and handed it to her. She opened slowly. It was the picture of Roman, Asher, and Gentry—the one where Gentry was sitting by himself.

Roman cocked his head and gave her a sad smile. "We need to redo this one. Do you want to take the picture?"

She was so overcome with emotion, her answer stayed stuck in her tightening throat. She nodded instead.

Roman pressed his lips onto her forehead and made his way to the big rock with his brothers. Blaire gave her an emotional smile, tears rimming her happy, green eyes. This was a big moment for the Strikers.

Asher sat in the snow, Roman beside him, and right beside Roman sat Gentry. All three looked out over that gorgeous sunset and waited as Mila clicked picture after picture on the camera.

Roman turned and gestured to her. "Come here."

"Okay," she whispered. When Blaire hugged her as she passed, Mila almost lost it. How many moments had they spent like this as kids and had taken them for granted?

Mila sat beside Roman, leaned against him,

resting her head on his shoulder. He settled his cheek on her hair. She could feel him smiling, and she closed her eyes as the sunset warmed her cheeks. The clicking of the camera faded away as she melted into this beautiful moment with the man she loved. With the man she had always secretly loved. With the man who now loved her back.

"Mila, open your eyes," Roman said. His voice sounded strange, nervous almost.

When she opened them, Gentry wasn't sitting beside her anymore, and Asher wasn't sitting on Roman's other side. She twisted around to see where they'd gone, but they were standing with Blaire behind the camera.

Confused, she looked back at Roman, but he was holding something. It was a small white-gold band with a single diamond that glittered like the snow. Mila clamped her hands over her mouth as tears filled her eyes. Couldn't be.

Roman said, "Mila, it was always you. You were the light. You were the only one who was going to save me, the only one who had a shot at keeping me steady. My little chicken." A grin stretched his face. "I got to watch you turn into a big bad wolf, and I'm so fucking lucky you picked me back. Plus, you have"—his eyes dipped to her cleavage—"perfect ten tits."

"Roman, focus," Blaire said through an emotional laugh.

"Right. Mila, you're already my mate. You're already my home. Wherever you go, whether you stay here in Rangeley or want to travel the world, I'll go. I'll do whatever makes you happy because your smile is where I feel okay. Will you marry me?"

Mila closed her eyes tight, dislodging tears as her shoulders shook with emotion. "Yes," she squeaked out.

"Yes?" Roman asked, lifting her chin with his finger. "For real? You're saying yes?" he asked louder.

She laughed thickly and swallowed a sob. "For me, it was always you, too."

Roman swallowed over and over as he slid the ring on her finger, and then he pulled her in tight. Mila could hear the clicking of the camera. He'd done this so sweetly, at a place that meant so much to her, in front of the people she loved.

For the rest of always, she would never forget how utterly happy she was in this moment.

One by one, the others came and sat on the ledge

beside them—the Wolves of Winter's Edge.

On her right was her best friend, her mate, her fiancé, her future husband...her entire future. And to her left was Blaire, Gentry, and Asher, all staring out over the snow-covered hills with absent smiles on their lips.

Without warning, Asher tossed his head back and gave a long, low, haunting howl. Gentry joined, then Blaire. Roman was watching Mila, and he smiled knowingly as the urge to join them bubbled up inside of her. He leaned forward and kissed her lips softly, and then he arched back and howled, too.

Asher was calling something from her, some instinct to sing with them that was impossible to resist. So she didn't. She let off a howl with the four rogues who had made their way into her heart and encouraged her strength.

She let off a howl of joy for what she'd found in a town that had been immersed in darkness.

She let off a howl with her mate, her best friend, her Roman.

She didn't know what would happen as alpha, but she wasn't a Bone-Ripper anymore.

Mila was a Wolf of Winter's Edge.

Want more of these characters?

Roman is the second book in a three book standalone series called Wolves of Winter's Edge.

For more of these characters, check out these other books from T. S. Joyce.

Gentry
(Wolves of Winter's Edge, Book 1)

Asher
(Wolves of Winter's Edge, Book 3)

About the Author

T.S. Joyce is devoted to bringing hot shifter romances to readers. Hungry alpha males are her calling card, and the wilder the men, the more she'll make them pour their hearts out. She werebear swears there'll be no swooning heroines in her books. It takes tough-as-nails women to handle her shifters.

Experienced at handling an alpha male of her own, she lives in a tiny town, outside of a tiny city, and devotes her life to writing big stories. Foodie, wolf whisperer, ninja, thief of tiny bottles of awesome smelling hotel shampoo, nap connoisseur, movie fanatic, and zombie slayer, and most of this bio is true.

Bear Shifters? Check

Smoldering Alpha Hotness? Double Check

Sexy Scenes? Fasten up your girdles, ladies and gents, it's gonna to be a wild ride.

For more information on T. S. Joyce's work,
visit her website at
www.tsjoyce.com

Printed in Great Britain
by Amazon